"You'll want to be married for real one day, Suzie.

You're a woman who believes in marriage and happily-ever-afters. And children. And it will happen. When you find the right man."

Suzie couldn't look at him, afraid of what she might see in his eyes. Afraid of what her own might reveal. "Please, Mack, I don't want—" She stopped, taking a quick sharp breath. "*What are you doing?*"

"Just checking if your hair's dry." His hands were at her nape, his fingers threading through her curls. It was the lamest excuse she'd ever heard, but she didn't immediately jerk away, her skin tingling under his touch.

"Don't," she whispered huskily, but she still couldn't seem to move.

"He wasn't the man for you, Suzie. Trust me."

That made her jerk back away from him. "Trust *you?*" she breathed. "You'd be the last man I'd ever trust!"

Dear Reader,

The year is off to a wonderful start in Silhouette Romance, and we've got some of our best stories yet for you right here.

Our tremendously successful ROYALLY WED series continues with *The Blacksheep Prince's Bride* by Martha Shields. Our intrepid heroine—a lady-in-waiting for Princess Isabel—will do anything to help rescue the king. Even marry the single dad turned prince! And Judy Christenberry returns to Romance with *Newborn Daddy.* Poor Ryan didn't know what he was missing, until he looked through the nursery window....

Also this month, Teresa Southwick concludes her much-loved series about the Marchetti family in *The Last Marchetti Bachelor.* And popular author Elizabeth August gives us *Slade's Secret Son.* Lisa hadn't planned to tell Slade about their child. But with her life in danger, there's only one man to turn to....

Carla Cassidy's tale of love and adventure is *Lost in His Arms,* while new-to-the-Romance-line Vivienne Wallington proves she's anything but a beginning writer in this powerful story of a man *Claiming His Bride.*

Be sure to come back next month for Valerie Parv's ROYALLY WED title as well as new stories by Sandra Steffen and Myrna Mackenzie. And Patricia Thayer will begin a brand-new series, THE TEXAS BROTHERHOOD.

Happy reading!

Mary-Theresa Hussey
Senior Editor

Please address questions and book requests to:
Silhouette Reader Service
U.S.: 3010 Walden Ave., P.O. Box 1325, Buffalo, NY 14269
Canadian: P.O. Box 609, Fort Erie, Ont. L2A 5X3

Claiming His Bride

VIVIENNE WALLINGTON

Published by Silhouette Books
America's Publisher of Contemporary Romance

SILHOUETTE BOOKS

ISBN 0-373-19515-X

CLAIMING HIS BRIDE

This edition published by arrangement with Harlequin Books S.A.

Visit Silhouette at www.eHarlequin.com

Printed In U.S.A.

VIVIENNE WALLINGTON

is an Australian living in Melbourne, Victoria, in an area with lots of trees, birds and parkland. She has been happily married to John, her real-life hero, for over forty years, and they have a married son and daughter and five grandchildren who provide inspiration for her books. Vivienne worked as a librarian for many years, but was always writing as well, eventually having a children's book published. After two more years, she gave up writing for children to concentrate on romance. She has written nineteen Harlequin Romance novels under the pseudonym Elizabeth Duke, and is now writing for Silhouette under her real name. Her favorite hobbies are reading, research, family and travel.

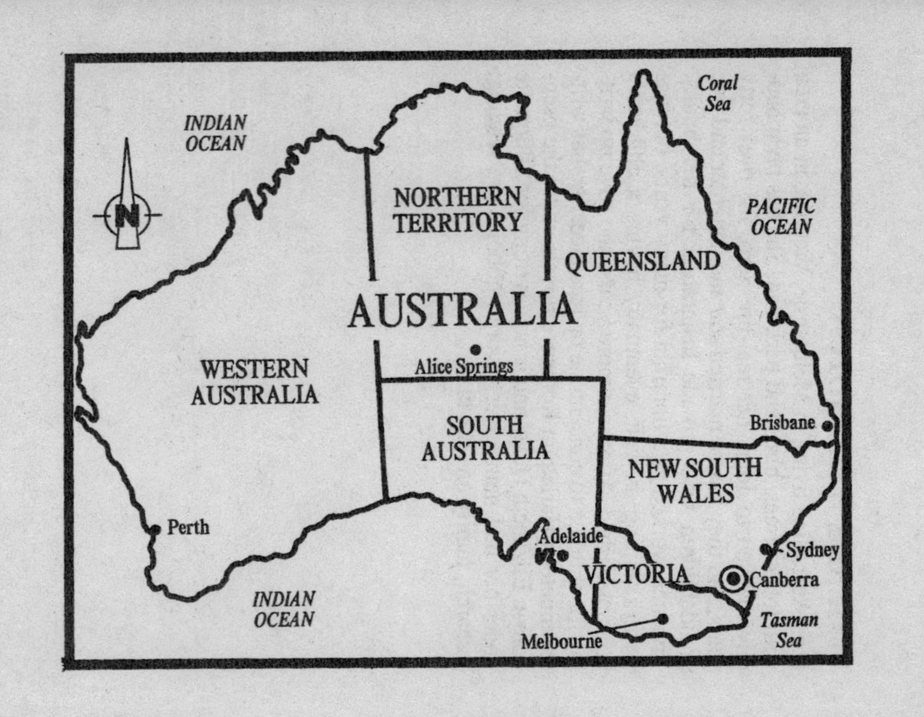
Coral Sea
INDIAN OCEAN
N
NORTHERN TERRITORY
QUEENSLAND
PACIFIC OCEAN
AUSTRALIA
Alice Springs
WESTERN AUSTRALIA
SOUTH AUSTRALIA
Brisbane
NEW SOUTH WALES
Perth
Adelaide
Sydney
VICTORIA
Canberra
INDIAN OCEAN
Tasman Sea
Melbourne

Chapter One

Sydney

"Wow, just look at all those cameras and photographers down there!" Ruth Ashton's eyes widened as she looked down over the sweeping lawns and gardens of Bougainvillea Receptions from the bride's dressing room. "And they've all come to see you, Suzie."

Her daughter was pirouetting in front of the full-length mirror, swirling the long skirt of her embroidered ivory lace wedding gown—one of her own designs. Suzie's sole bridesmaid, Lucy, in ice-blue silk, was fluttering around her, making sure everything was as it should be.

"They've come to see my wedding dress, not me—they want to see what fabulous design I've come up with this time." Suzie's voice shook a little. She'd wanted a simple, informal garden wedding, but it was fast turning into a media circus.

"Well, it's not every day a young fashion designer without her own label wins the prestigious Australian Gown of the Year award." Her mother's face glowed with pride. "Today's added publicity could really boost your career, darling. Fashion editors from all the top fashion magazines are here."

"I'm only allowing all those cameras and fashion sharks in," Suzie returned rather sharply, "to save Jolie Fashions, who've been so good to me. I don't want to see them go under." The Sydney-based fashion house was in severe debt and struggling for survival, thanks to a crooked accountant. "The media exposure will be great publicity for Jolie, especially with my bridesmaid and the bride's mother and the bridegroom's mother and a good proportion of the guests wearing Jolie designs."

"Darling, the fashion media will take one look at your fabulous wedding gown and fall over themselves to get pictures of you, and fashion buyers will flood Jolie Fashions with orders. Your wedding will feature in every top fashion magazine, giving Jolie all the publicity they could possibly need. And you, too, dear." Ruth's eyes misted. "You look divine, sweetheart. I've never seen a more beautiful bride. Tristan's going to be so proud of you."

Tristan. Suzie swallowed. Her golden prince. Gentle, steady, reliable, responsible, charming, successful—the perfect husband-to-be. He might not be a man to inspire mindless passion, but mindless passion was dangerously misleading, blinding one to reality. She would always know where she was with Tristan.

He was a man a girl could rely on, depend on, unlike…

She pushed the unwanted thought away, refusing to think of Mack Chaney on her wedding day. Or any other day, ever again. He was past history. And good riddance.

"You're going to make a perfect couple," Lucy said with a sigh. Tristan was so handsome, and so rich and Suzie, whom she'd known from their school days, had magically transformed herself from an unruly-haired imp into a regal, sleek-haired princess. "Just perfect."

Yes, everything was perfect…almost too perfect. Suzie felt a momentary qualm. It all seemed unreal, like a dream. A glittering Cinderella fairy tale. She'd never expected to find the perfect man. She'd never believed that a perfect man existed. The only men she'd been close to in her life had been anything *but* perfect.

She was anything but perfect herself.

She moved quickly across to the window, wobbling a little on her ivory satin high heels. She couldn't look at her mother or Lucy, afraid they might see the flare of guilty panic in her eyes, the flickering fear that she was about to be exposed as a fraud.

Tristan didn't know her at all. Not the real Suzie—the scruffy, impulsive, slapdash Suzie. He only knew the elegant, coolly composed, immaculately groomed Suzanne, as he preferred to call her—the sedate, ladylike image she'd been trying so hard to keep up for the past three months—with her mother's encouragement.

From the moment Suzie had caught the eye of the young leather-goods tycoon at the Australian fashion awards three months ago, her mother had been determined not to let Tristan get away. Even Tristan's mother, the snobbish Felicia Guthrie, had come to accept her future daughter-in-law, despite Suzie's modest upbringing and unexceptional background.

It would have helped, of course, that Suzie had recently won the Gown of the Year award. She was now *somebody.* A talented young designer with a bright future.

Suzie's mouth went dry as she saw the huge crowd gathered in the garden below. As well as the rows of seats for the invited guests, which were filled already, there was a milling mob behind, with a daunting sea of cameras and giant zoom lenses, all waiting to see her latest spectacular design.

She nervously fingered the long sleeves of her elegant lace gown and the tiny pearl beads scattered over the tight-fitting bodice with its dropped waistline, then let her hand flutter down over the flared skirt.

Her natural curls were nowhere in sight, skillfully straightened into gleaming sleekness, the way she'd worn it for the past three months. On her head she wore a small pearl tiara, with a gossamer-sheer veil. Nothing must hide or detract from her wedding gown.

"Where's Tristan?" She swung around, her voice higher than usual. "It's the bride who's supposed to be late, not the bridegroom." Not having a father to give her away, she'd decided to walk into the garden arm in arm with her future husband.

"He's not late," her mother soothed. "He'll be here any minute."

Lucy ran to the door and peeked out. "He's coming up the stairs! Are you ready, Suzie?"

"As ready as I'll ever be." Suzie gulped in some air. Once she saw Tristan, once he smiled at her with his golden smile, she would feel a whole lot better.

He entered the room a few seconds later, a picture of sartorial elegance in formal white, his golden hair burnished by the crystal chandelier above. Outside, in the bright afternoon sunlight, it would gleam even more.

"Suzanne...you look like a dream. A princess."

As she felt the warmth of his golden smile and saw the loving pride beaming from his gentle gray eyes, her qualms slipped away. She was going to have a very safe, secure and tranquil life with Tristan. Peace, security and contentment were what she longed for after the fights and frustrations and wildly swinging emotions that she and her mother had had to endure with Suzie's charming, talented but totally irresponsible father.

The kind of life Suzie would have had to endure with Mack Chaney if she'd been mad enough to give in to her foolish passion for him.

Getting tied up with Mack long-term would have been a disaster. The Mack Chaneys of this world weren't cut out for a secure, settled, pipe-and-slippers kind of life—the kind of life *she* wanted. All Mack cared about was speeding around on his Harley-Davidson and playing with his computer, idly surfing the Internet and dreaming wildly impractical dreams—pie-in-the-sky pipe dreams. She shut her mind to his other vices.

"Are you ready to go down?" Tristan asked, and she jerked herself back to earth. This was the most important day of her entire life and she was thinking of—

No, she *wasn't.*

She let Tristan steer her toward the door, but they never reached it. Someone burst through the doorway first.

Suzie's eyes widened in disbelief when she saw Mack Chaney bearing down on her like an avenging angel—or devil—in a black leather jacket, tight-fitting black leather pants, and black boots. His dark eyes were glittering with purpose and his thick black hair was as wild and untamed as it had always been.

"You're actually intending to marry this pampered fraud?" he barked, halting abruptly in front of her. "I never thought you'd go ahead with it, Suzie. I thought you'd see the light long before today."

"How *dare* you burst in here and—" Suzie stopped. "What do you mean—*fraud?*" She glared at him.

"Get him out of here!" sputtered her mother. "Call security!" she commanded Lucy.

"Wait!" Mack held up a hand. "You can't marry Tristan Guthrie, Suzie. Not if you want your marriage to be legal!"

Suzie felt Tristan's body shudder against her and heard her mother's sharp intake of breath. She glanced up at her shocked bridegroom, but he didn't meet her look, or make any move to draw her into the comforting protection of his shoulder, not even offering her a reassuring hand. Shock seemed to have robbed him of movement—and of his voice. His stunned gaze was transfixed on Mack Chaney's dark-eyed, ruggedly good-looking face.

Suzie's mother stepped forward, her face contorted in fury. "You'd try anything, wouldn't you, Mack Chaney! I always knew you were trouble!"

Mack's darkly sensual mouth curved a trifle. "I think the fact that Tristan Guthrie is already married justifies my presence here."

Suzie swayed, feeling faint. It was Mack whose hand shot out to steady her, not Tristan's. Tristan was still frozen and speechless with shock.

"Is this some kind of sick joke?" she hissed at Mack as the faintness began to recede and anger took over. It wouldn't be the first time Mack Chaney had played a practical joke on her. But never one like this. Never one so cruel.

"Why not ask your bridegroom?" Mack suggested, his tone derisive.

"I don't need to," she retorted. "It's laughable." But Tristan wasn't laughing. Nobody was laughing. And no wonder. This was outrageous! "You've obviously made a mistake. Or made it up!" Her scorn lashed Mack, hiding a growing apprehension. Why was Tristan being so quiet? Why wasn't he denying it? Getting mad? Demanding that Mack Chaney be thrown out?

"Tristan, tell me it's not true." Her eyes sought her bridegroom's face. The clean-cut, perfectly sculptured features were ashen, his long-lashed gray eyes stricken. Would he look so pale and shocked if it wasn't true? "Tristan..." Her eyes caught his, pleading with him. "Tell me he's wrong."

Tristan found his voice at last, a hoarse croak. "Of course he's wrong." He turned accusing eyes on Mack, but there was little fire in the gray depths, and his voice shook as he demanded, "Where's your proof? You've been listening to malicious idle gossip."

"It was a piece of idle gossip that led me to check

up on your past,'' Mack rasped. ''It didn't take long to uncover your shabby secret. You married a woman ten years ago while you were a student at university, and you've never obtained a divorce!'' He pulled some papers from his pocket. ''Here's a copy of your marriage certificate, and confirmation in writing that no divorce has been filed.''

Lucy gasped. Tristan's pale face seemed to crumple. He cast an anguished look at Suzie's mother. No sympathy there. Just fury, shock and disbelief.

Tristan turned back to his stunned bride, brushing Mack Chaney aside to seize her hand. ''We can work this out,'' he promised hoarsely. ''I'll fix it.''

''You mean it's *true?*'' Suzie recoiled. Tristan had a wife he was still married to, and he'd kept it from her? Her perfect, high-principled, reliable Tristan had *lied* to her? *Deceived* her? That realization was almost as bad as knowing that her bridegroom was married and contemplating bigamy! She'd always thought Tristan so honest...so upright...so honorable.

Still reeling, unable to believe it, she asked carefully, spelling it out to make doubly sure. ''You married another woman ten years ago and you're still married to her?''

Tristan began to bluster. ''It was never a real marriage, I swear it. Love never came into it. It was purely a—'' he hesitated, his handsome face contorting in guilty anguish ''—a marriage of convenience,'' he mumbled, so low she could barely hear. ''She was a foreigner—an overseas student—who wanted my help to stay in Australia. I was doing her a *favor,*'' he asserted lamely. ''We married in secret and kept it quiet. After a few months we split up and went our separate ways.''

"And where is she now?" Suzie forced out the question, feeling sick. If today's wedding had gone ahead, she wouldn't have been Tristan's legal wife. She would have been married to a bigamist! And wasn't it an offence, she wondered dazedly, to marry under false pretences, the way Tristan had? How could he be so dishonest and unprincipled! How *could* he?

Tristan wrung his hands. "I don't know where she is. I heard the year after we...married that she'd left Australia and gone to some remote part of Africa to be a missionary or something. So much for wanting to stay in Australia!" He gave a disgusted snort. "I tried to trace her to send divorce papers, but she'd vanished from the face of the earth. Nobody knew where she'd gone. I've never heard anything of her since. She's probably dead," he said with a dismissive toss of his golden head.

"You would have been notified if she was dead," Mack interjected coldly. "As her husband, you're her next of kin."

Next of kin... Suzie felt dizzy. No words could have made the nightmare more real.

"I'll find her, darling." Tristan gripped her arm. "I'll get a divorce. We've been apart for years, so even if I can't find her, there should be no problem...."

She looked up into his pale, handsome face, at his quivering jaw, at the long-lashed gray eyes that couldn't quite meet hers, and saw him for the first time as he really was. A shallow, spoiled, weak-willed fraud, just as Mack had said.

"How could you, Tristan?" she cried. "How could you keep a thing like that from me? From the woman you say you love and want to marry and share your life with!''

''I—I'd forgotten about it,'' he said weakly, but one look at his face was enough to tell her that was patently a lie. She wondered if he'd ever made an effort to find his wife, or if that was a lie, too. ''It was so long ago, darling...we were just kids. Impetuous young students. It never meant anything...I hardly knew her...and now...well, she left Australia years ago, so why drag it up again?''

Suzie gave a choked cry. ''Because you're still *married* to her, Tristan.... Don't you understand?'' He still didn't accept that he'd done anything wrong. He just wanted to shut it out of his mind and blot it out of his pampered existence as if it had never happened.

Oh, Tristan, she thought with a despairing sigh. I don't know you at all. And here I was, feeling guilty about you not knowing the real *me!*

''Just go, Tristan.'' She couldn't bear to see the pained, self-righteous hurt in his eyes, or to listen to any more of his blustering self-justification. ''I would never marry you now, whether you had your divorce or not.''

''I suggest,'' Mack drawled, ''that you go down to your mother, Tristan, and quietly lead her out of the garden, along with your closest relatives, to save them the embarrassment of a public scandal.''

Tristan's stricken eyes flared in relief. ''Yes, yes...thank you, I will.'' He slunk out with a hoarse apology, his eyes avoiding his bride's, as if too ashamed—or not brave enough—to meet her withering gaze.

Coward, Suzie thought, profoundly relieved that

Mack had saved her from marrying such a lily-livered weakling—though she wished it had been anyone else but Mack Chaney who'd come to her rescue!

"Oh, darling, run after Tristan," her mother pleaded. "Can't you go ahead with the wedding and worry about..." Her voice trailed off as she caught the scathing contempt in her daughter's eye. "Well, at least give Tristan a chance to—to extricate himself from this embarrassing—"

"Mum, I could never marry him now," Suzie said flatly. "How could I ever trust him after this? After hiding a thing like an existing *marriage* from me? I thought he was a man of honesty and integrity. I th-thought he was perfect."

She heard a snort from behind, and scowled. Mack was enjoying all this, no doubt...acting the big hero...sweeping to her rescue in the nick of time....

"Nobody's perfect, darling," her mother said pensively. "There's good and bad in everybody. You'll never find a perfect man. But Tristan is more perfect than any man you're likely to meet." She shot a virulent look at Mack. Ruth had never approved of Mack. "And he loves you."

"Does he?" Suzie asked dully. Were a few chaste kisses a measure of a man's love? Had *she* ever truly loved *him?* Or had she simply been dazzled by his golden looks and comforted by the thought of a calm, secure future?

"Well, what are you going to *do?*" her mother wailed. "Everyone is down there waiting for you, dear. All those cameras and fashion experts...all desperate to see your bridal gown and to feature your wedding day in their magazines. And Jolie Fashions are relying on you, darling, for the publicity. For their *survival!*''

''And what about all the food and champagne?'' Lucy piped up. ''You can't waste it!''

Suzie's head was spinning. The dream she'd thought so unreal had turned into a nightmare that was only *too* real. What *could* she do? There was no way she was going to run after Tristan and beg him to go through a sham wedding ceremony with her...no way in the world! Not even to save Jolie...

Pain pierced her at the thought. Jolie Fashions had taken her on as a struggling fashion student and given her time off to continue her course, even paying her study fees. They'd given her a job as a junior designer, and encouraged her to enter the Gown of the Year with her own design. She owed them everything!

''Suzy, remember what Jolie have done for *us*...for me as well,'' her mother appealed to her. ''You *must* go after Tristan.''

The sight of her mother's distress wrenched Suzie's heart. Jolie Fashions had been wonderful to her mother, too, taking her on as a dressmaker at a time when she'd desperately needed paid work. Ruth had supported Suzie through the long dark years, while she was still at school. How could she stand by and watch Jolie go under, taking her mother with them? Without her wealthy clients at Jolie Fashions, Ruth would have to struggle, all over again.

As she stood hesitating, Mack spoke up again.

''There is a way out.'' His dark gaze pinned hers. ''You could marry *me*, Suzie.''

Chapter Two

"We have special permission," Mack was quick to assure her. "The celebrant already has the documents. They only need your signature, Suzie."

She stared back at him, too stunned to think of asking how he'd wangled special permission. The black eyes piercing hers were deadly serious. If this was one of Mack's practical jokes, there was no sign of it.

"We can go down into the garden now," Mack continued coolly, "get married in front of all your friends and that media pack waiting for you, Suzie, soak in all the publicity you need to save your fashion house and to hold up your head as a rising star of fashion design, and we can dissolve the marriage afterward, if that's what you want." He glanced at Suzie's mother.

Ruth's eyes wavered. She knew all about holding up one's head. She'd been keeping up appearances all her married life...making out that her marriage was a normal one, that her husband wasn't the useless no-hoper he'd become. To have to stand by and watch her daughter marrying Mack Chaney would be intolerable, but if they planned to dissolve it afterward...

"But what would we *tell* everyone?"

"Just tell them your daughter realized she couldn't go through with her wedding to Tristan Guthrie and decided to follow her true heart," came Mack's drawling response. "You can always tell them later it didn't work out." *If he could win over Suzie's mother...*

Ruth looked as if she'd swallowed a lemon. "I meant what would I tell them about *you?* Everyone knows my daughter would never marry an aimless, unemployed biker!"

Suzie's head swam. Their voices seemed to be coming from far away. *Her true heart?* Was she dreaming...or paddling through a nightmare?

"Just tell them I'm in computers," Mack advised easily.

Ruth sniffed. "You can't get married in black leather!"

"The fashion world will *love* a bridegroom in black leather," Lucy interjected, excitement bubbling in her voice. "It's so romantic!"

Ruth pressed a hand to her chest. "But why does it have to be *you?*" she croaked, glaring at Mack.

Mack clenched his jaw. "I guess because I was the only one who thought to check up on Tristan Guthrie. And because I care about what happens to your daughter, Mrs. Ashton."

"And you think my daughter wants to get tied up with *you?*" Ruth's eyes flashed daggers at him. "She doesn't! She's made that quite clear in the past." She gulped down her anger, her gaze sliding away. "But if you're serious about this being only a temporary arrangement...and if my daughter agrees..." To save face...to save Jolie Fashions...to save her daughter's career...

"Well, Suzie?" Mack turned to his prospective bride, who'd remained silent until now. She'd been *shocked* into silence. "It's your call."

Suzie's head was still spinning. It was impossible to think straight. Her mother's bitter attack on Mack a second ago had had a curious effect on her, making her feel almost *defensive* of him, tempting her to point out his good points to her mother. Only with her mind in such a tumultuous state, she couldn't think of any! She'd spent so much time over the past three years reminding herself of Mack's many faults...his many sins...trying only to think of *them*...

Mack watched the conflicting emotions in her eyes and relaxed a trifle. She was coming around...it was going to be easier than he'd thought.

"Mrs. Guthrie's leaving!" Lucy reported from the window. "So are the people she's sitting closest to. There's no sign of Tristan...he must have sent one of the staff to speak to his mother."

Tristan hadn't even had the courage to face his mother himself? How pathetic he was, Suzie thought in disgust. What a lucky escape she'd had...and such a *close* escape...and she could thank Mack....

Her eyes clouded. She didn't want to be indebted to Mack Chaney.

Mack felt a tinge of anxiety. He'd seen that look before. *Don't get cold feet now, Suzie.* "I promise I'll give you your freedom afterward, Suzie, the moment you ask. I'll sign anything you want me to." His eyes burned into hers, challenging her—even as he held his breath.

As Suzie stared back at him dazedly, her mother spoke up again, Mack's promise reassuring her. "Suzie dear, if you're going to go ahead with this wedding, we'd better get moving. The celebrant will be waiting downstairs. You'll have to brief her of any changes you want..."

"She'll think we've gone mad," Suzie said faintly.

Mack's dark eyes glinted. She was actually going to go ahead with it! He hid his relief. "Mad *about each other,*" he corrected smoothly, trying to curb his impatience. He didn't want her backing out now....

"I'll go down to the garden and let people know that you're coming." Ruth was already moving toward the door. "I can just imagine their shock, Suzie, when you turn up with an unruly-haired biker in black leather instead of Tristan Guthrie!"

"They'll only have eyes for the bride," Mack murmured, "not for the man by her side."

"Oh yeah?" Lucy breathed, eyeing him avidly. Mack was far more romantic, in his dangerous, brooding sort of way, than the impeccable, golden-haired Tristan, who'd turned out to be a bit of a wimp.

Mack held out his hand to Suzie. "Shall we go down?" He gave her a rallying smile.

The sight of his smile reassured Suzie as nothing else could. This was what she'd dreamed of once...walking down the aisle with Mack Chaney...before she'd realized she would never be able to rely on him...that he wasn't the responsible, settling-down type.

But she didn't have to worry about the future. They

wouldn't be married long enough. She could believe in the dream and just for today *live* the dream.

She took his hand and smiled back. A smile she knew she must keep up for the rest of the afternoon.

Somehow she managed it, but her head was still whirling and she was barely conscious of her feet touching the ground. She was barely conscious of anything, except vague impressions.

The official wedding photographer waiting at the foot of the stairs, the marriage celebrant coming forward to discuss the service and deal with the necessary paperwork, the barrage of cameras as she and Mack stepped out into the sun-drenched garden, the sighs of admiration as her bridal gown was duly inspected and approved and finally the stunned faces of the guests as she walked between them with Mack by her side, Lucy following close behind.

They exchanged vows in front of a shady gazebo, with Mack producing a wedding ring which, he confided, had belonged to his mother. Mack had been close to his mother, so the ring would mean a lot to him. Suzie was touched by the gesture.

"I do," she heard herself answering when the time came, and suddenly she was married, and everyone was waiting for Mack to kiss her. He did....

The cameras went mad. As a newlywed couple, they had to sign more documents at a table in the gazebo, before enduring another barrage of photographs, not only from their own official wedding photographer, but from the clamoring fashion media. The guests, many resplendent in Jolie fashions, were also photographed. Suzie's bosses were ecstatic.

It was a relief to finally escape the media circus, the bridal couple retreating with their guests to the reception house, where the media weren't permitted. But they had their pictures and went away happy, dispersing quickly, keen to be the first with their fashion scoop.

As the guests spilled into the various rooms of the brightly lit, flower-bedecked reception house, champagne and appetizers were served, and the noise level rose. Everyone was having fun, the mood heightened by the astonishing turn of events.

Tristan and his mother had wanted a formal reception, but Suzie had insisted on a party instead, with a smorgasbord-style buffet set up in one of the rooms and a towering profiterole dessert instead of a formal wedding cake. A jazz band was playing in the conservatory, and some of the guests were dancing already.

"Can't we get out of here?" Suzie begged Mack as they moved from room to room, neatly avoiding probing questions. A good few of the guests were Tristan's friends, who'd stayed on out of curiosity. "I want to go home. You must want to escape, too. Nobody will notice we've gone. With all these rooms, we could be anywhere."

"Fine with me." Mack's dark eyes were unreadable. "We'll slip out the back way. But you'd better let your mother know."

"I guess so. You wait here." Suzie dashed off, weaving through the crush until she found her mother, flopped in an armchair. "Mum, I need to get away from everyone. I'm exhausted. I'm going to slip away."

Her mother nodded in sympathy. "I'll come home with you," she offered. "You must need a comforting shoulder to cry on after all that's happened."

Suzie hid her alarm. The last thing she wanted was her mother's sympathy—especially if she started commiserating about Tristan! She immediately changed tack. "Mum, Mack and I are going to have a quiet drink somewhere away from all the fuss. I'll be home later tonight," she promised. "I've no intention of spending the *night* with Mack," she assured her mother, who nodded in relief.

"Don't wait up for me," she added, and fled.

Moments later she was out in the floodlit courtyard with Mack. The cool air hit them in the face. The afternoon had been sunny and mild—a perfect autumn day—but now it had clouded over, with one ominously dark cloud directly overhead, and there were already a few spots of rain.

She looked round. "The wedding car's not here," she groaned. "It must be round the front."

"You won't need the wedding car." Mack was ushering her toward a big gleaming black motorcycle.

She balked. "I'm not riding on that thing. I hate motorbikes."

"You loved riding with me once."

"That was before—" She stopped, a deep shudder quivering through her. *Before her father had crashed his high-powered Harley into a power pole.*

"I know, Suzie, and I'm sorry about your father, but you'll be safe with me, I promise."

Safe with Mack Chaney? When had she ever been safe with Sydney's wild-boy bachelor?

Only he wasn't a bachelor now. He was her husband. She began to tremble. Reaction was setting in.

As she stood hesitating, Mack's fingers closed over her shoulders—warm, strong fingers that sent a tingling heat through the delicate lace. "You know what they say when someone falls off a horse.'' His voice held a seductively persuasive note—a familiar note that brought back disturbing memories. ''Get right back on and get rid of the demons.''

She looked up into his compelling black eyes and shivered, her mouth twisting. The only demon she had to fight was Mack himself. She'd been fighting that particular demon for the past three years, and for another year before that, when they'd been together—on and off. When Tristan Guthrie swept into her life three months ago, she thought that she'd finally succeeded in ridding herself of the demon that was Mack Chaney.

Tristan. Her golden prince. Her charming, sensible, honorable, dependable, perfect... Pah! She should have known he was too good to be true. Hot tears pricked her eyes.

''You want to get away from here or not?'' Mack was already mounting his shiny black Harley and waiting for her to make up her mind.

''Yes, get me away! But I—I've decided not to go home yet. Mum will be home shortly, and I just can't face her again tonight. Let's have a quiet drink somewhere.''

''We'll go to my place. Hop on!''

His place? But she hardly cared where. She just wanted to get away from here, before someone saw them and tried to drag them back inside.

She looped the long skirt of her wedding gown over her arm—she'd discarded her veil and headpiece earlier—and jumped up behind Mack. He'd pulled his helmet on and had unhooked the spare one for her.

''Here, put this on,'' he ordered, thrusting it at her, but she gave a reckless shake of her head.

"I want to feel the wind in my hair. I've a lot of cobwebs to blow away."

"It's illegal not to wear a helmet," Mack reminded her with rare deference to the law. She laughed—a brittle, almost hysterical laugh. Illegal? *Bigamy* was illegal! Not wearing a helmet was hardly the crime of the century. But she took it and rammed it on her head. "Come on, are we going or not?"

"We're going." Mack revved the engine. "Hang on!"

She did, clinging to him for dear life as his high-powered machine sprang forward and roared off down the sweeping driveway to the street. The spatters of rain were increasing, great splashing drops now, gathering momentum by the second.

She shut her eyes, relishing the wind and rain in her face because it gave her something else to think about other than the shocking events that had taken place at Bouganvillea Receptions.

She could feel her carefully straightened hair sprouting curls as the rain seeped under the helmet. Well, it hardly mattered now. Tristan wasn't going to see it. Mack, on the other hand, was bound to make some cutting remark about her new look—her artificial new look—when they finally reached the sanctuary of his home.

Sanctuary? A shiver feathered down her spine. By running off with Mack Chaney, wasn't she jumping out of the frying pan into the fire?

As they careered round the first corner, Mack suddenly nosed his bike into the kerb and brought it to a halt.

"What are you doing?" she cried as he eased himself out of her grasp and leapt off.

What he was doing, she realized, was peeling off his leather jacket. He had a plain black T-shirt underneath which emphasized the breadth of his muscled chest and exposed the impressive muscles of his tanned arms. She pursed her lips, wondering if he'd added workouts in the gym to his other leisure activities.

"Here. Slip your arms into this." He helped her into his jacket, which was several sizes too large for her, but felt beautifully snug and warm. "It might protect you a bit."

Surprised at his unexpected gallantry—but then, Mac had always been a man of surprises, good and bad—she showed her gratitude with a light, "Thanks, Mack. Now *you'll* get wet through."

"Never mind about me," Mack muttered as he threw a sturdy thigh over his bike and settled back into his seat. There was an edge of mockery in his voice, as if to say, *When have you ever minded about me?* "Ready to go? Hold on, Suzie!" The big machine shot forward.

The rain was tumbling down. She could feel her wet curls clinging to her cheeks, her neck. She thought of Tristan and her mouth dipped. What would it matter now if she reverted to her natural curls and dropped her sophisticated, ladylike facade? Who was going to care now that her golden prince had turned into a tarnished frog?

Just as her dark prince had, three years ago.

She wondered bleakly if an honest, dependable man existed anymore.

She turned her face into the driving rain, as if that

might wash them both out of her mind and out of her life. But it was pretty futile when she had her arms around the dark prince, his ring on her finger and would shortly be arriving at his home.

Chapter Three

As Mack swung his bike into the narrow driveway of his modest weatherboard home, which he'd inherited from his mother about five years ago, Suzie felt herself trembling again. Not with reaction this time, or even with cold—Mack's jacket had saved her from catching a mortal chill—but with a shivery apprehension.

She'd been to Mack's house a few times during the roller-coaster months they'd been together—or more accurately, *seeing* each other. They'd never actually been together in *that* sense, though it had come close a few times and would undoubtedly have happened if Mack hadn't shattered her faith in him—albeit blind, rebellious faith—by showing that he possessed the same destructive traits that had wrecked her father's life.

Her mother had mistrusted Mack from the start and warned her to keep right away from him. Suzie had known in her heart that Ruth was right about him, that he was the last man in the world she should be seeing, let alone falling for, but try as she might she hadn't been *able* to keep away from him. Until that awful night three years ago—the night Mack had demonstrated, with painful clarity, that he was no different from her father.

Disillusioned, she'd refused to see him again, refused his phone calls, even refused to speak to him when he'd turned up at her father's funeral a few months later. She'd wanted to make it clear to Mack that whatever they'd shared together was now dead, and that she was severing all connections with him.

"We're here now, Suzie, you can let go of me," Mack drawled, and she realized they'd pulled up near his front steps and that she was still clinging to him. She released him as if her hands were suddenly on fire, and scrambled off the big machine, groaning as she looked down at her mud-spattered ivory satin high heels and the soaked skirt of her elegant wedding gown.

"My dress and shoes are ruined!" she moaned. "Haven't you ever thought of buying a car?"

"And give up my Harley?" Mack grinned at her through the rain. In the glow of his porch light, drops of water beaded his heavy eyebrows and thick lashes, giving his dark eyes a pearly sheen. "Come on inside, Suzie, out of this rain. We'll have to get these things off. We're both soaked." His wet T-shirt clung to his muscled chest like a second skin.

We'll have to get these things off? Alarm shot through her. "I'll be fine," she babbled, wondering why she'd ever agreed to come to his home with him. Was she mad? This wasn't a real marriage, for heaven's sake! They'd agreed it wasn't going to last.

"Your jacket has kept me nice and dry and warm," she mumbled.

"Only the top half of you." He was still grinning, damn him, as he surveyed her sodden gown and shoes. "But I can't see your wedding dress surviving somehow. I hope you're not having second thoughts about marrying Tristan when you're both free again, assuming he ever gets his divorce, of course!"

She almost snapped back, "No, I'm not!" but she caught the words back, scowling instead. A bit of doubt on Mack's part might be a good thing. As a protective device. Mack had supreme powers of persuasion, as he'd demonstrated before when she'd been determined to keep away from him. Until he'd shown his true colors on that last soul-destroying night, and she'd made it quite clear to him that he was out of her life for *good.*

But she still wasn't immune to him, she realized in dismay. Not entirely immune. Having to keep her body pressed up against him all the way to his home, and her arms wrapped tightly around him, had shown her that. The feel of his taut muscles under her hands had sent her heartbeat haywire and her pulses soaring, and even now she could still feel her nerve endings twitching. She would have to be well and truly on her guard against him, every second she spent with him.

As Mack whisked her up the rickety front steps to the shelter of his small covered porch, she fingered her wet tangle of curls and wondered ruefully what Tristan would have thought of her smooth, sleek hair sprouting rebellious curls before his eyes. Would he have laughed, and loved her just as much? Or would he have sent her off to have her hair professionally, *permanently,* straightened?

She simply didn't know. What madness had made her want to rush into marriage with a man she didn't really know? A man she'd only known for three months?

It had been nothing but a dream. And dreams weren't real. Fairy tales weren't real.

She heard a thud, and then another, and realized that Mack was tugging off his boots. As he peeled off his socks, revealing dark-skinned bare feet, she gulped and looked away, kicking off her own mud-spattered satin shoes.

Mack unlocked his front door and waved her in. "I'm glad to see your curls are back, Suzie," he commented as he led her into the front room—a combined sitting room and workroom—and switched on the overhead light. Only one of the three bulbs was working—typical of Mack Chaney, Suzie thought, glancing upward. On her past visits here, he'd often overlooked practical household basics, his mind too absorbed, no doubt, with the Internet and his latest brilliant idea.

But at least the lighting was softer than it would have been with all three bulbs working!

"What on earth did you do to your hair before?" Mack asked, fingering a stray damp curl. He was thinking how cute she looked with her wet curls clustered round her cheeks, and how dewy and moist and kissable her lips looked, and how she'd die if she knew she had mascara running down her face. "And why?"

Suzie jerked her face away. "I needed a change." No way would she tell him the real reason she'd dispensed with her curls—to impress Tristan Guthrie on the night of the Gown of the Year awards. Tristan, as head of the Guthrie Leather Goods empire, one of the sponsors for the event, had presented the main award.

Knowing he'd be there, her mother had urged Suzie to make an effort to look more elegant and sophisticated in the hope that her daughter would catch the eye of the eligible young bachelor. Dolled up in her award-winning gown, with her new sleek hairstyle and ladylike demeanor, Suzie had done her mother proud. Tristan had had eyes for no one else all night—or for the following three months.

"I had it straightened, that's all," she said with a shrug. "Every woman likes a new look occasionally."

"Why change what's perfect already?"

A tremor quivered through her. Mack was the only one who'd ever thought her perfect as she was. Everyone else preferred her new sleek-haired, sophisticated look—her mother, her workmates at Jolie Fashions, Tristan, his snooty mother.

"And you don't need all that eye makeup and mascara," Mack chided. "You're too fair. It looks unnatural."

"Tristan liked me like this." He'd never taken a second look at the natural Suzie. He'd come to Jolie Fashions once to pick up his mother after a fitting, and he'd walked straight past her without a glance.

"He should have liked you as you really are."

She twitched a shoulder. *He never noticed me as I really was.*

Mack reached up to brush a finger over her cheek. "Your mascara has run," he mocked softly. "The hazards of makeup. Still, I'm sure Tristan appreciated your glamorous new look." His dark eyes taunted her. "He'd like the cool, sophisticated ice-maiden look, from what I found out about him. Nothing too hot or passionate or unbridled for our straitlaced golden boy.''

He was so close to the mark that she forgot she hadn't intended to let him get under her skin, and she lost her cool. ''From what you *found out* about him?'' she lashed back. ''I still can't believe you actually had the nerve to check up on my fiancé's past—just on a vague, spiteful hunch!'' She was too incensed to acknowledge that if he hadn't, he would never have discovered and exposed Tristan's secret marriage, and she would be the wife of a bigamist by now.

''There was nothing spiteful about it. I was merely looking out for your welfare. But we can discuss your errant ex-fiancé when you have a soothing drink in your hand. And when you've removed those wet things.''

She flinched away from him. ''Oh...you mean your jacket.'' She hurriedly slipped it off and handed it back to him. ''Thanks.'' She paused, glancing down. ''I don't suppose it matters that I'm leaving muddy splotches and watery drops on your carpet. How long since you've had it cleaned? Sometime last century?'' She screwed up her nose in distaste at the stained, threadbare carpet.

''Oh, that old thing, it'll be going soon.''

Yeah, I'll bet, Suzie thought. And pigs might fly. She was still frowning at the carpet. ''What did you do—hold a wild party in here? What are these stains—red wine? Or did someone get stabbed?''

His lip quirked. ''It's grease. I took my bike apart in here and made a bit of a mess.''

She rolled her eyes. ''Heavens, Mack,'' she exclaimed, looking around the room properly for the first time, "this whole room's a mess. It's a disgrace."

There were piles of papers and cardboard cartons stacked on the floor, and more cluttering the tables and desktops, where a computer and keyboard were just visible. The armchairs had newspapers and computer magazines strewn all over them. "Don't you ever tidy your house? Or do any cleaning?"

"I've been busy. I'm not going to die because of a bit of dust or a few messy papers and boxes. Besides, nobody sees the mess but me."

"*I'm* seeing it."

"Since when did a bit of mess bother you, Suzie?" His dark eyes glinted. "There was a time when you only noticed *me,* and the chemistry that flared between us every time we looked at each other. And we had more than just chemistry going for us."

Suzie wanted to stop him, but his next words brought such nostalgic memories flooding back that they formed a lump in her throat, making speech impossible.

"Remember how we used to love listening to the band concerts and feeding the pigeons in Hyde Park, Suzie? And watching the yacht races on Sydney Harbour at weekends? And how we loved a good joke? And talking about everything under the sun? Music, sports, politics, books, movies, our dreams, our ambitions?"

She unlocked her throat. "Pipe dreams, in your case!" Her heart rate had picked up to a disturbing degree at his reminder of three years ago, and scorn seemed the best way to cover her turmoil. "You were always full of talk about what you were going to do with your life when your brilliant ideas hit the jackpot and you made tons of money, but I don't see any sign that you've become rich and famous in the past three years!"

She raked a disparaging look around. "Nothing's changed, has it, Mack? When I first met you, you'd just thrown in a perfectly good job and dropped out of university, and you've never knuckled down to a proper job since as far as I can see—let alone hit a jackpot!"

No, nothing's changed, she thought, stifling a sigh. He's just like my father. All *his* dreams of becoming rich and famous—in his case with his paintings—had come to nothing, too.

Mack gave a snort. "What was the point in staying at uni? I knew more about computers and programming than my lecturers. And the job I had with that computer firm was leading nowhere. And I *have* been working since then. Every time I sit down at my computer I'm working."

"Playing games," she scoffed.

"Inventing *new* games," he corrected. "New programs. New software."

"That nobody's interested in!"

She would never have been so harsh or so discouraging three years ago—she would have put his failures down to being ahead of his time and urged him to keep trying—but she was still bitter at the way Mack had killed her trust in him on that last traumatic night, revealing a side of him she'd never seen, and never wanted to see again.

"So little faith!" Mack sighed. He seemed amused rather than devastated, she noted in exasperation. "How you've changed, Suzie. You encouraged me once."

"Until I realized you were just like my father…living on your dreams and never facing reality," she retorted. Didn't he even *care?* "You're going to end up just like him, with nothing to show for your life." *And look what that had done to her father.*

"Is that why you cut me out of your life as if I'd never existed?"

She avoided his eyes. She'd never told him the full extent of her father's sins. She'd only mentioned his depression, his drinking and the frustrations of a brilliant artist with a tortured soul. Both she and her mother had always tried to cover up her father's destructive gambling, to protect the self-esteem of the man they'd both loved to the end. Loved, hated and despaired of.

"I was only nineteen," she defended herself. "I was still a student. I had my career to concentrate on. I—I didn't want to get involved with—with anyone."

"Especially not with me."

"All right—especially not with you! And you were never really *in* my life, so stop twisting the facts. We were never *together.* We were just friends."

"Do you kiss all your friends with the passion you used to kiss me?"

The memory of their passion—the wild, steaming passion that had flared between them every time they'd looked at each other, every time they'd touched, and especially when they'd kissed—brought a remembered heat to her body. She seized on anger to douse it.

"How dare you throw my adolescent mistakes back at me, today of all days! And it was only a few kisses. You make it sound as if it were a grand passion." Damn it, it was once…to her. It could have been—if he'd been less like her father, if he'd been able to resist the temptations her father had succumbed to. She could still see the elated look in Mack's eyes the night he'd come home from the casino rolling in money and reeking of whiskey. She blinked the bitter memory away.

Something shimmered in Mack's dark eyes, but he said nothing, moving to a corner cabinet to extract a half-empty bottle of Scotch and two glasses. Suzie compressed her lips. So he still drank whiskey!

He poured some into both glasses and handed her one. "Here, sip this while I fetch you something to change into. I don't possess a dressing gown, but I might have a tracksuit that'll do. You'd better have a hot shower and get out of that wet garb before you get pneumonia."

He strode from the room before she could argue.

She took a gulp of her whiskey and coughed. She hated whiskey and rarely touched it, remembering what alcohol had done to her father. And Mack could end up the same way, if he kept on drinking. But this, she told herself, was medicinal! She took another more determined gulp, taking comfort from the hot spirit as it coursed a fiery path down her throat.

Mack came back as she was about to take another reviving sip. He hadn't wasted time changing and was still wearing his wet T-shirt and black leather pants.

"Here. This will have to do." He handed her a gray tracksuit. "It has a drawstring waist, so you should be able to keep the pants up."

She had a strange sense of déjà vu. Mack had been wearing a similar gray tracksuit—maybe even this one—the day she'd first met him. Like most things about Mack, their meeting had been dramatic and unconventional.

Her boss had sent her to a house in Mack's street to deliver a new outfit to a client. She'd borrowed one of the company cars, which she wasn't familiar with. Worse, it was a manual, not an automatic. As she was about to drive off after making the delivery, she'd reversed the car by mistake and had collided with Mack as he careered out of his front gate on his Harley—far too fast to stop in time, and looking in the opposite direction.

It was only a glancing blow, but Mack had come off his bike and crashed to the pavement. She'd jumped out of the car and rushed to him, her heart in her mouth, horrified to see blood all over his face. It was only a nosebleed, she'd discovered, but at first glance it had looked far worse. She'd insisted on taking him inside his house to tend to his wounds.

He'd been more apologetic than she had, berating himself for not wearing a protective helmet. He'd only been planning to ride up his street and back, he'd told her ruefully, to test some work he'd just done on his bike.

He'd been lucky. Very lucky.

So had she. Her stupid mistake could have killed him!

"Suzie?" Mack's voice penetrated her musings, and she realized he'd just said something to her.

"Oh, sorry. What did you say?"

"I just said, you know where the bathroom is." His dark eyes seemed to swallow her up, as if he were remembering their first meeting, too.

He turned away to pick up the glass of whiskey he'd poured for himself, tossing the contents down at a gulp, bringing a frown to her brow as the devil-may-care action reminded her of her father's reckless drinking.

"I'll change while you're showering, Suzie," he said as he led the way, "and then I'll make us some coffee."

She opened her mouth to tell him not to bother about coffee, that she wouldn't be here long enough, but she snapped her mouth shut again. Where would she go? She couldn't go home yet—her mother could be home by now, and she didn't want to face her mother again tonight. She didn't feel up to fielding questions or dealing with sympathy.

Mack certainly wouldn't be offering her any sympathy.

He didn't. His first words, after they'd settled into armchairs in the front room—she noted he'd removed the newspapers and magazines while she was in the shower—were, "What were you thinking of, Suzie, getting mixed up with a pampered pussycat like Tristan Guthrie? The jerk has no conscience and no backbone—obviously. And he's never worked for anything in his life, as you must know—he inherited his money *and* his business success. He didn't have to lift a finger."

His voice dropped to a husky drawl. "As for passion—I don't think he'd know the word, would he?"

As her breath caught, he leaned forward in his chair, his coffee mug cradled in his hands. He'd changed into faded blue jeans and a black polo shirt, which made him look marginally less tough than his black leather gear, while just as disturbingly masculine. But what he was saying was even more disturbing. She didn't want to talk about passion!

"You must realize what an escape you've had, Suzie. Tristan Guthrie would have bored you to death. He's far too weak and wishy-washy for a passionate—" he paused as Suzie's eyes flew to his, sparking with hot blue fire. "—sorry…for an independent, strong-minded woman like you," he amended.

"Is that why you checked up on him?" she snapped. "Because you thought he wasn't right for me and you hoped you'd find some embarrassing skeleton in his closet?"

He didn't deny it. "He struck me as too smooth, too smug, too picture-perfect. He didn't ring true. I decided to dig around a bit and find out more about him."

"You must have dug really hard…and deep…and low." Her eyes told him just how low she thought *him,* for thinking of delving into her fiancé's past in the first place—rightly or wrongly. Who did he think he was? Her keeper?

"I did. I checked records, spoke to people and finally found one of his fellow university students from ten years ago who mentioned this foreign woman he was with for a while. I delved a bit deeper and picked up rumors of overseas students marrying secretly to stay in the country. I thought it was worth following up. I examined marriage records, and bingo! Tristan Guthrie, large as life. But there was no record of any divorce."

He settled back in his armchair with a satisfied smirk. Then, as if the whole sordid scandal was now explained, dealt with and behind them, he commented easily, "I'm glad to see you looking yourself again,

Suzie. The curls, the natural face. You don't need all that artifice and makeup. You're beautiful without it. And I must say you look very fetching in my track-suit.''

Did she realize, he wondered, that it was the same tracksuit he'd been wearing when she'd knocked him off his bike on the day they first met? Not just off his bike—she'd knocked him off his entire axis. Through a whirl of stars, he'd found himself drowning in the bluest eyes he'd ever seen, eyes full of anxiety and compassion—for *him.* And when she'd opened her mouth to speak, his bedazzled gaze had settled on full, lush lips that had begged to be kissed—only he'd been in no position to kiss them, with blood pouring from his nose and a throbbing pain in his head.

Once she'd helped him inside, mopped him up and made him feel half-human again, she'd gone back to work—but not before he'd asked if he could call on her later to thank her properly. He still remembered the way she'd blushed and nodded.

Yeah, he'd been smitten all right. And not just by her looks. Young and innocent as she'd been, she'd possessed a maturity and a toughness beyond her years. He'd sensed hidden depths and hidden pain, yet her natural humor, her cheeky wit, kept bubbling to the surface.

Everything about her fascinated him. She was a heady mixture of mystery, allure, vulnerability, ambition and an awesome inner strength that he suspected had something to do with her home life, which he'd gathered had been pretty rough. She'd never liked to talk about it, though she'd dropped the occasional hint now and then—usually at times when she flounced out of his life, comparing *him* with her no-good father.

He and Suzie had had more breakups in the months they'd been seeing each other than he could remember. And just as many reunions—until she'd walked out on him for good, without a proper explanation.

And now here she was, back in his life again. *Married* to him, while it lasted. Whether it did or not could be up to him.

"Mm...*very* fetching," he repeated, unable to take his eyes off her.

Suzie shivered under the hot sweep of his gaze. "Oh, sure." She gave a snort, but she could feel her cheeks heating, her skin prickling under the gray fabric. "It's about a mile too big and I've had to roll up the sleeves and the legs several times and they're *still* too long. But at least I'm dry."

"You look gorgeous. And naturally beautiful." *Suzie, baby, you'd look good in a sack,* he thought, and found himself wondering what she'd look like in nothing at all. He quenched a sharp stab of desire and made an effort to steady his voice. "You'll be much happier being yourself again, Suzie, not some untouchable ice maiden."

Untouchable? Suzie's heart jumped. What had made him say that? Did he *know?* She bowed her head over her hot coffee. *Don't be silly, how could he possibly know?*

"I left my wedding dress on your bathroom floor," she mumbled. Anything to switch the subject! "You might as well throw it out. It's ruined now."

"Well, it's served its purpose. And knowing you fashion designers, you'll want a new up-to-the-minute model if and when you ever decide to get married again...for keeps.'' His dark eyes caught hers for a challenging second.

''At this precise moment, I can't imagine wanting to be permanently married to anyone, *ever,*'' she said fiercely, with a shudder.

Mack repressed a sigh. So, after all his efforts to save her from Tristan Guthrie and win her back, she still didn't want to be married to him. At least not beyond tonight. But things could change. ''Oh, you'll want to be married one day, Suzie. You're a woman who believes in marriage and happily-ever-afters. And children. And it will happen. When you find the right man.'' *When you realize you've already found him.*

Suzie couldn't look at him, afraid of what she might see in his eyes. *Or afraid of what her own might reveal.* ''Please, Mack, I don't want—'' She stopped, taking a quick sharp breath. *''What are you doing?''*

''Just checking if your hair's dry.'' His hands were at her nape, his fingers threading through her curls. It was the lamest excuse she'd ever heard, but she didn't immediately jerk away, a strange languor sweeping over her, her skin tingling under his touch. *Tristan* had never run his fingers through her hair.

''Don't,'' she whispered huskily, but she still couldn't seem to move, or twist her head round to shake him off.

''He wasn't the man for you, Suzie. Trust me.''

That made her jerk back away from him. ''Trust *you?*'' she breathed. ''You'd be the last man I'd ever trust!''

She gulped in a rallying breath. He was waiting for her to crack, to admit that his presence disturbed her.

Waiting for her to throw herself back into his arms and confess how she'd missed him and how badly she wanted him back in her life, regardless of his faults and failings.

Well, you'll be waiting, she vowed hotly. She'd had a lifetime of pain and disillusionment to harden her heart against irresponsible charmers like Mack Chaney and her father. She'd watched her mother being worn down, day after day, and had sworn she'd never end up like her.

Mack looked pained. "I saved you from marrying a potential bigamist, didn't I?"

She scowled. "I suppose you expect me to be grateful to you." Her voice trembled. "Well, all right, I'm glad you found out in time. B-but you had no right to interfere in my life. You should have asked someone else to check up on Tristan." Anyone else!

"I thought I had the right as a friend, Suzie. Friends look out for each other."

"A *friend?*" Her eyes seared his. "We haven't been friends, or even spoken to each other, since—" She stopped, shaking her head. Since the night he'd come round to her place boasting of his big win at the casino, thinking she'd be happy about his stroke of good fortune and *congratulate* him.

"Since the day of your father's funeral," Mack finished for her, reminding her that he'd turned up unexpectedly on that somber occasion, a few months after their abrupt parting.

Suzie took a gulp of her coffee. Her mother had kept her closely under her wing from the moment Mack had shown up, so that he would have no chance to speak privately to her, except to offer his condolences to both of them. She'd turned sharply away from him afterward, making it plain that she wanted nothing more to do with him.

Any man so like her father! It would be disastrous to get involved with Mack again. *He'll end up the same way as your father, one of these days,* her mother had warned her over and over again, and despite the feelings she still had for Mack, she'd known that Ruth was right.

Mack had taken the hint and kept out of her life after that, and a few weeks later she'd heard that he'd gone off to travel round Australia on his Harley-Davidson—a trip that could have lasted months or years. She wondered when he'd come back. Just as well he had! Nobody else had thought to check up on Tristan Guthrie's past.

"It must have been tough, finding out that your bridegroom had a wife already," Mack conceded, his voice a warm, deep rumble, "but you don't seem too heartbroken, Suzie, I'm glad to see. You know in your heart, don't you, that Tristan was wrong for you?"

His assumption that she wasn't heartbroken and—even worse—that he knew what lay in her heart, raised her hackles. Silvery-blue sparks flashed in her eyes. How would Mack Chaney know anything about what was in her heart or what she was thinking? She hardly even knew herself!

Chapter Four

She set down her coffee mug with a thud and rose abruptly from her armchair, to begin a restless prowling among Mack's stacks of papers and cartons.

"I suppose it's lifting these boxes and piles of junk that's given you all those muscles, Mack," she quipped, anxious to talk about something—anything—other than herself or Tristan.

"You noticed my muscles?" There was amused irony in his voice, as if he were thinking, *If you were heartbroken over Tristan, you wouldn't be noticing another man's muscles.* "Actually, I was getting a bit out of condition, spending so much time sitting at the computer. I thought I'd better work out a bit to keep fit."

"You've been going to the gym?" she asked sweetly, but her thoughts weren't so sweet. So he was admitting that he still spent most of his time in front of a computer! It was on the tip of her tongue to ask him why he didn't find a proper job, but she bit the words back, not wanting to show any personal interest in him. Their marriage was a sham, never intended to be a real marriage…a lasting marriage.

"Yeah, now and then. You should join me sometime."

Her heart jumped. He spoke as if they had a future together! She moved swiftly to the fireplace to avoid his probing gaze. The open grate was jammed with papers, not firewood, and the mantel above was a jumble of photographs, computer discs, cards and envelopes.

A framed photograph caught her eye. It was a family portrait of a mother, a father and two children, a boy and a girl. On past visits here she'd seen photographs of Mack with his mother and younger sister, now married and living in New Zealand, but she'd never seen any photographs before of his father. She'd presumed there weren't any—or they'd been thrown out. Mack had always refused to talk about his father, except to growl that he'd walked out on his family when Mack was ten and his sister eight.

"Your father, Mack?" she asked, curious to know why he'd put the photograph on display, after ignoring his father's existence for so long. Had Mack finally forgiven his father? Finally decided to acknowledge him?

She was still facing the mantel and failed to see or hear Mack step over to stand behind her. *Close* behind. Then she didn't need to hear him, or see him, she could *feel* him with every fiber and nerve ending of her quivering body! It was almost a physical impact, the pulsing waves between them so strong they raised goose bumps on her skin.

This is ridiculous, she thought, refusing to believe

that Mack could still affect her in such a way. In such a *sensory,* spine-tingling way. She must be suffering some emotional reaction after all, she decided shakily, from the stressful events of the day.

"Everything's not always as it seems," Mack said from behind, and she turned then, her curiosity piqued. Her breath caught in her throat as she found herself a heartbeat away from his lips. Lips she still dreamed about at times, before waking up trembling and sweating and wondering how she could possibly still retain such disturbingly vivid images of him when she had Tristan in her life now.

Or she *had*...until a few hours ago.

"What do you mean?" she breathed, wanting to step back, away from him, but unable to move with him so close and the fireplace jammed up behind her.

Instead of stepping back himself, Mack slipped his hands over her shoulders—not in a rakish, suggestive way, but resting them heavily, as if he had a weight on his mind—almost as if *he* were in need of support. But that was silly. Mack wasn't the type of man to need support from anybody.

Shivering under his touch, acutely aware of the strength and warmth of his fingers, she flicked a glance up at him—but the brooding black eyes were looking beyond her, a haunted light in their depths.

"My father wasn't the heartless deserter my mother and I always thought him." His tone was as heavy as the hands on her shoulders.

Her eyes widened. "Tell me, Mack," she urged softly, her curiosity and compassion for Mack overcoming—well, *almost* overcoming—her shivery reaction to his touch. His hands were still clamped over her shoulders, as if he still needed her support, or was it simply physical contact he needed?

"The early years of my childhood were happy enough." Mack was staring past her again, his jaw clenched as if he were determined to hide any emotion. "Dad couldn't have been a more loving husband or father, but around the time I turned ten, he began to change. He became moody and self-absorbed and difficult to live with. Then one day, out of the blue, he lost his job. He'd worked for the railways all his life and had always been highly regarded by everyone, so it came as a huge shock."

She saw a pulse throbbing at his temple and her heart went out to him. "Did they tell him why?"

"He told my mother he'd been retrenched because they needed to cut down on staff. But later on we learned the truth. He'd lost his job because his work had slipped and he was making too many mistakes."

"Oh. Was he able to find another job?"

"He didn't seem interested. His moods grew worse, his behavior more erratic and confused—he just wasn't his old self at all. At first Mum put it down to him losing his job. Luckily she already had a part-time job at a café and was able to increase her hours to keep us going. But after a few more weeks of his strange, moody behavior, Mum began to suspect he was having an affair."

"And was he?"

"She never asked. Before she could confront him, he walked out on us. He left a note saying he didn't want to be married anymore and we were to forget him." Mack had thought as a boy that his father had rejected *him,* that he must have done something bad. When, years later, Suzie had rejected him, too, it had brought the old remembered pain flooding back, so that losing her was even harder to bear.

"Oh, Mack, how awful for you!" Suzie longed to reach out to him. "And for your mother. I suppose she assumed he'd run off with someone else."

Mack grimaced. "What else could she think? She never spoke his name again after that. She disposed of his personal possessions and hid away all his photographs, and it was as if he'd ceased to exist. A few months later the police came to tell us he'd been killed in an accident. He'd been struck by a truck on a busy city street. My mother didn't even go to his funeral. She was afraid the other woman might be there."

His shoulders lifted and fell. "Life went on, and about five years ago my mother died, too. Of a broken heart, I reckon. And overwork." His voice roughened, the memory still painful. "She'd taken on two jobs to feed and educate us kids and help us through university."

"And you dropped out!" Suzie blurted out before she could stop herself.

Mack's gaze pierced hers. "I dropped out of a *computer* course I was doing at uni, *two years after my mother's death.* I'd already done an accounting and business degree a few years before that."

"Oh." Suzie flushed. "And you finished it?" Oh heck, why had she asked *that?* What would pop out of her mouth next? But how could she think rationally when he was so suffocatingly close? When his hands were still grasping her shoulders, their warmth seeping into her skin. When she could barely even breathe.

She would have done anything for some air, but if

she pushed him away, or tried to break away from him, this rare moment might be lost. Mack had never opened up like this before, and she wanted to hear more, though heaven knew why. She didn't want to connect emotionally with Mack Chaney. No way. That would be stepping onto far too dangerous ground.

"Yes, Suzie, believe it or not, I did finish it," Mack replied dryly.

Her flush deepened. "You said something about things not being as they seem," she reminded him. "What did you mean by that?"

His expression sobered. "About a year ago, out of the blue, a letter arrived, addressed to my mother, with an apologetic note from a doctor's surgery. The letter was from my father. He'd written it shortly after he walked out on us—years ago!—and left it at the surgery with instructions to deliver it to his family after his death."

His chest heaved. "But somehow, through some bungle, Dad's letter was buried under papers and forgotten—" he tossed a rueful glance around at his own mess as if he understood perfectly how that could happen, "and it wasn't discovered until last year, when the surgery's files were cleaned out and replaced by computers."

"At his *doctor's* surgery," Suzie pursed her lips. "Are you saying…?"

"I'm saying that my father had found out, before he walked out on us, that he was dying. But not of a simple, quick, easily treated disease. He'd found out that he had early-onset Alzheimer's disease." Mack spoke in an even, matter-of-fact voice, but Suzie sensed the anguish underneath and her heart nearly burst for him.

"He knew that he was already deteriorating rapidly, and would continue to go downhill," Mack said heavily, "and that he'd end up being unable to do anything for himself and becoming a burden to his family, perhaps for years."

"Oh, Mack!" Her hand rose instinctively to his face, letting her sympathy flow into his roughened skin through her fingers. "*That's* why he left home? To save your mother the worry and torment of having to look after him, having to watch his inevitable decline?"

Mack nodded, a brooding glitter in his eyes. "Knowing my mother, she would have been happier taking care of Dad, no matter how long and difficult the task, than she ended up being, living the rest of her life without him, imagining that he'd stopped loving her and had run off with another woman."

Tears welled in Suzie's eyes. How tragic that his mother had died before her husband's letter had been delivered to her. Her own troubles paled in comparison. "Perhaps he *wanted* your mother to hate him," she ventured, "so that she would get on with her life. And possibly meet someone else..."

Mack's powerful shoulders hunched. "Well, she never did. She never wanted anyone else. She never loved anyone but my father...even though she never mentioned his name again. She died with a broken heart."

Suzie couldn't bear to see the pain in his eyes. "Maybe he thought that was kinder than her dying of a broken spirit after watching him suffer year after year. Or her ending up resenting him for wrecking her life and becoming a burden to her.''

The brooding black eyes met hers. ''Maybe. I only know that Dad sacrificed everything that was dear to him out of love for my mother and for his family. He loved us. I realize that now, though it's too late for my mother, unfortunately.''

''Thanks to his doctor's surgery not delivering his letter.'' Suzie sighed. If his mother had received the letter immediately after her husband's death, she would have known that he still loved her, and would undoubtedly have gone to his funeral and cherished his memories for the rest of her life.

It was heartbreaking! But at least Mack—and presumably his sister in New Zealand—knew the truth at last.

''You must be relieved, Mack,'' she consoled him, ''to know that your father didn't linger on for years, unable to function properly and perhaps not knowing anyone around him. Far kinder, perhaps, that he died a quick, merciful death the way he did—in an accident.''

''If it *was* an accident,'' Mack said soberly. The words hung in the air for a poignant moment. ''Yes, of course I'm relieved. And I know my mother would have been, too. Perhaps they're both reunited up there somewhere.'' He flicked a brief glance upward.

''I'm sure they are,'' Suzie said passionately, wanting to believe it more than anything. Her eyes had filled with tears again, and Mack bent his head and pressed his lips to first one damp eyelid, then the other.

''You weep for my parents,'' he murmured, ''but

there were no tears for yourself and Tristan, Suzie. I find that interesting.''

She blinked rapidly, her brow darkening at his reminder of the fairy-tale wedding that had turned to bitter dust. ''I don't want to talk about Tristan,'' she growled. ''I never would have come here with you if I'd known you'd keep bringing up his name.''

''My apologies.'' His hands dropped from her shoulders at last, leaving a cold emptiness in their place. He reached for the family photograph on the mantel behind her. ''I've tried to make amends to my father by retrieving any photographs I could find, and letting Dad's old friends and workmates know about his illness. Better late than never,'' he said, his tone rueful.

''Your parents were a handsome couple, Mack,'' Suzie commented. She was gazing at the portrait in his hand, at the man who'd sacrificed everything for love, and the woman who'd never mentioned her husband's name after he walked out on her, but who'd kept all his photographs and had never looked at another man since. ''Your mother was a real beauty, with that lovely pale skin and fair hair, and her sweet smile. She's like an English rose.''

''Only much tougher,'' Mack murmured, his eyes softening. He'd always spoken fondly of his mother, never hiding how grateful he was for the sacrifices she'd made for him and his sister. It was something Suzie had always liked about him.

''And your father...'' She hesitated, her cheeks heating. He looked so much like Mack! How could she rave about his father's rugged good looks and striking black eyes when Mack must be aware of the startling similarities between father and son? ''He looks a fine, upright man, Mack,'' she said carefully. And then, with no caution whatsoever she added, ''You might take his example and get your hair cut occasionally!''

His eyes swung around to meet hers, darkly amused. ''You think my hair's too long?'' He fingered his damp mass of black hair, which curled over his ears to his shoulders. She couldn't imagine him with short hair—or maybe she could, now that she'd seen a photograph of his father. He'd look like his father. Almost respectable.

But she couldn't imagine Mack looking respectable, either—or even wanting to. And in a way, despite its wildness, she *liked* his hair long. She always had.

She realized he was waiting for an answer and cursed herself for ever mentioning his hair. Getting personal around Mack Chaney was like stepping into a field of land mines. She gave a careless laugh and tried to sidestep neatly away, wanting to put space between them. But she tripped over a heavy carton of papers and went spinning to the floor before Mack could do a thing to save her.

Sprawled on the threadbare carpet, she groaned and started rubbing her elbow.

''Suzie, are you okay?'' Mack tossed the family portrait into a chair and dropped to his knees beside her.

''It's my funny bone.'' And don't you dare laugh, she thought, it's not funny. ''I hit it on the corner of your damned desk as I fell.'' She groaned again, rubbing madly.

''Here, let me help.''

''No, I—'' She stopped, suddenly losing her voice as she found herself pressed up against his chest, cradled in his arms. How had *that* happened? One of his hands was pushing hers aside and taking over the rubbing of her painful elbow.

"Ouch!" she squeaked, but his hands were warmer and far more soothing than her own had been, and she could feel the pain ebbing away as if by magic. She stayed where she was, enjoying the sensation of comfort, and feeling snug and warm in his arms. His *lethal* arms…

She knew just how lethal they were—they always had been—but she had little fight at the moment, after learning the truth about Tristan—and the tragic tale of Mack's father. And the whiskey she'd gulped down earlier had weakened her defenses even more.

She allowed herself to sink back in his arms.

"Were either of your parents Scottish, Mack?" she heard herself asking curiously.

"No, why?" He sounded bemused.

"I just wondered. How did you come by the name Mack? What's it short for?"

"It's not short for anything. It was my mother's maiden name. She was Katherine Mack before she married my father."

"Your mother's maiden name, what a lovely idea. And your sister's name is what? Katherine?" A smile tweaked her lips.

He laughed. "No, her name's Belinda—after nobody in particular. My mother just liked it," he said with a jerk of his shoulder, making her very conscious of the shifting muscles of his chest.

"Oh." Her voice was suddenly husky. "Well, Belinda's a pretty name."

She knew she shouldn't be lying here in Mack's

arms, but it felt so good, so comforting. She didn't think about what else it was doing to her. Or what ideas it might be giving *him*. None, hopefully. She'd had enough drama for one day!

The computer on his desk caught her eye. She didn't use a computer herself, and often wondered how it could be so endlessly fascinating to some people. She only knew how time wasting and beguiling it could be. As tempting as gambling, as addictive as alcohol—and perhaps, ultimately, as soul destroying?

She thrust Mack's obsession from her mind and dragged her thoughts back to his father. A far safer topic!

"I'm glad you finally learned the truth about your father, Mack. Now you can put all those painful years behind you and start remembering the good times you had together, before he fell ill." A pensive note crept into her voice. "You must have lots of happy memories of your childhood. Of the early years."

His rough jaw brushed her temple. "Are you speaking from your own experience, Suzie?"

His shrewd perception brought a wary gleam to her eye. She and her mother had always tried to hide her tormented father's more serious problems, implying that his troubles arose from his genius as an artist and having to deal with setbacks and disappointments.

How much Mack actually knew or had guessed she couldn't be sure, and she didn't intend to ask or enlighten him now. It would only draw attention to Mack's own problems. Dismayingly similar problems. And she certainly didn't want to get into those!

"I have very happy memories of my childhood," she assured him, and she did, of her early childhood at least, before her father's downward spiral began.

"I loved my father," she asserted. But many times, in those long harrowing years, her love for him had been buried deep, almost lost under her pain and disillusionment.

And Mack Chaney, she must keep firmly in mind, was just like her father. Mack, as her mother kept on reminding her, would never amount to anything. He would end up drinking and gambling and idling his life away...and probably kill himself on his motorbike one day, just as her father had.

She shuddered in Mack's arms.

"I know you loved him, Suzie," Mack murmured, putting her tremor down to the memory of her father—not realizing, thankfully, that she was thinking of *him.*

Her breath caught as he cupped her chin with his hand and tilted her face so that he could look into her eyes. His own eyes were a dark, unfathomable glitter in the wash of the soft overhead light.

"It seems we both have a debt to pay to our mothers." His voice rumbled from his chest—the hard-muscled chest still pressed warmly up against her. "They kept our families afloat through some pretty tough times, and worked their fingers to the bone for us. I only wish my mother were still here, so that I could have a chance to do a few things for *her* in return."

There was such genuine regret in his voice that she bit back the words that leapt to her tongue: *What could you do for your mother? By the look of this house, you can barely even support yourself!*

Instead, in a rush of sympathy, she found herself curling an arm around his neck and kissing him lightly, impetuously, on the lips. "I'm sure your mother would have expected nothing from you in return, Mack,'' she assured him. ''Nothing but your love.''

It was a mistake. A big mistake.

Suddenly the atmosphere changed. Whether it was the word *love* spoken aloud, or her flippant, reckless kiss, or the way Mack had stilled, looking down at her in that dark brooding way of his, she couldn't have said. She only knew that sizzling electric charges were darting like tiny fireballs between them, that the air had filled with a breathless suspense, and that nothing, not even her awareness that she'd made a mistake, was going to save her.

She was being swept inexorably into the dangerously exciting place she hadn't wanted to go, and should be strongly fighting against.

Chapter Five

When Mack's mouth took possession of hers, every thought in her head evaporated, all her senses focusing on the exhilarating reality of his kiss, on his scorching lips, his roving tongue and the wild sensations burgeoning inside her.

Powerless to prevent it, she felt her own lips responding, answering his need with a burning need of her own. No other lips but Mack's had ever made her feel like this. No other man's kisses had ever driven her into such a mindless frenzy of passionate longing. Even though she'd known from her first date with him that it was madness to go on seeing him...that she must never let his kisses go too far.

And somehow, in the past, she'd always managed to draw back from the brink in time, by remembering her mother's warnings and her father's tormented, self-destructive existence. And, by reminding herself of the peaceful, stable, independent life she'd mapped out for herself.

Love isn't enough, her mother had drummed into her for as long as she could remember. *Never marry a man for love alone. Find a man you can respect and trust, and who will be able to provide for you and your children, not drag you down and break your heart and spirit.*

But this time, even knowing her mother was right, she knew she didn't want to stop, that she was incapable of stopping. She didn't have the strength, the willpower, the desire to fight him. Not tonight.

The desire...

She moaned, the very thought sending a spasm of white-hot longing through her. His own body shuddered in response, the heat of his skin like fire under her hands, even through his black shirt, already hot and damp from his sweat.

Wrapped in each other's arms, they writhed and rolled on the stained, threadbare carpet, their mouths still locked in an endless kiss, their hands wildly clutching, digging, clawing as their bodies arched and twisted. A blind, searing passion, tumultuous in its intensity, had possessed both of them.

"I've missed you, Suzie," Mack gasped against her lips.

She made a plaintive sound in her throat as she realized how much she'd missed him, too, even without knowing it—or only knowing it subconsciously, in her dreams...the dreams that had haunted her nights for the past three years. Awake, she'd refused to even think about him. She'd foolishly imagined, when she became involved with Tristan, that she was finally over Mack, that at last she could wipe him out of her life, out of her heart and out of her dreams.

But the perfect, trustworthy Tristan had let her down. The one man she'd thought never would.

She clung to Mack, kissing him back with equal fervor, wanting oblivion, wanting what she'd always longed from him, deep in her heart, body and soul, but had always fought against, knowing it could lead nowhere, except to ultimate disaster.

Who would have thought it would be her relationship with the flawless Tristan that would end in disaster? It just proved that nothing was sure in this life.

A raw moan slid from her throat. Why not follow her heart for once? Live for the moment, forget logic, forget common sense, forget there would never be a rosy future ahead for her with Mack Chaney. She was nearly twenty-three years old, for heaven's sake, and Mack was the only man she'd ever truly loved, ever truly desired—physically and emotionally. Mack wanted her and she wanted him. Oh, *how* she wanted him!

Love isn't enough, she could hear her mother warning her, but she wasn't planning a future with Mack, this was *now,* tonight, not the future. And for tonight she could live the dream and imagine their marriage was going to last….

A pile of papers tumbled down on top of them but they were barely conscious of them as their rocketing passion engulfed them, their moans and gasps mingling with the sound of the rain still thudding down outside.

"I've been waiting all my life for this—for *you,*" Mack groaned, and she uttered a tremulous sigh, wondering if she had, too. Right now, she didn't care about her mother's warnings, or about what happened in the future, she only cared about this moment and these *feelings.*

"Let me feel you, Suzie, and see you. All of you." Drawing her up onto her knees, Mack tore off his own shirt first, before reaching for the loose tracksuit top she was wearing, and pulling it over her head. His warm palms slid over her skin, below the scrap of ivory lace—her bridal bra—she was wearing underneath.

"Mm, your skin's like silk. You feel so good. And you smell so good, you always did. Sweet and spicy, like a field of wildflowers and exotic spices." Breathing heavily, he reached around behind her, his fingers fumbling with the fastening of her bra, thrusting it aside. As she wriggled out of the rest of her clothes, he tore off his.

He gazed at her for a long moment, his breath hissing from his lips, his eyes a dark glitter in the swirling gloom.

"You're beautiful, Suzie," he murmured hoarsely, clamping her to him, skin on skin, crushing her breasts against the damp heat of his chest.

Her own hands were doing some exploring of their own, digging into his back and shoulders, which felt every bit as good, the taut muscles smooth and hard beneath her fiery palms.

"Oooh!" Her body arched instinctively as he released her just far enough to gather her breasts in his hands, kneading them in a way that nobody—not even Tristan, *least* of all Tristan—ever had. When he found the taut peaks and began to rub gently, erotically, she cried out again, the riotous sensations driving her wild.

A groan tore from Mack's throat. He'd dreamed of

holding her like this, touching her like this, hearing her cry out like this...for *him.* He bowed his head and drew a sensitive tip into his mouth, exalting as she arched and cried out again.

Tearing his mouth from her breast, he sought her lips once more, his arms sweeping around her, lowering her to the floor, half fearing that any second she would wake up to what she was doing and roll away from him. Afraid that the dream would evaporate, as it always had before. He mustn't let it happen, he couldn't bear to lose her again, not now that he had her back in his arms where she belonged.

Suzie found herself lying flat on her back again on the carpet, with Mack on top of her, raining kisses over her face and throat. A consuming fire was burning her up, every nerve ending of her body achingly alive, every fiber of her being crying out for him, needing him, *wanting* him, as she'd never needed or wanted any man before.

She moaned softly, straining against him, prepared to go wherever he wanted to take her, and Mack seemed just as eager to take her there, his kisses scorching over her throat, her breasts, her stomach, before he pressed his body down on top of her, grinding his hips over hers, and driving her even wilder.

"Are you sure you want this, Suzie?" It was a hoarse growl, his body throbbing with his need, his passion at flash point, ready to explode.

"Yes!" she cried, clinging to him, not caring about the consequences, only about Mack, and how much she needed him. "Yes!"

Mack gave a low growl and let his blazing passion spiral out of control, plunging her into a whirlwind of sensation that hurtled both of them to explosive heights that neither had dreamed possible.

Suzie lay on the threadbare carpet with a smile on her lips and warm tears on her cheeks. She'd never dreamed that anything could be so earthshakingly wonderful. She remembered crying out at one point as a brief pain stabbed her, but the waves of bliss that had followed had blotted out that momentary discomfort—and everything else.

How would she ever be able to leave Mack now, never to hold him again, never to kiss him again, never to know this soul-lifting passion again? She loved him. She'd even told him so! She flushed as she recalled the way she'd cried out her love for him in those final moments. Would he remember? Throw her words back at her? Or did all women cry out, *I love you,* at the dizzy heights of passion?

Love is not enough....

Wasn't it? Right now, it felt more than enough. More than she could ever want, or ever need.

As she looked up and saw Mack gazing into her face, her flush deepened. Why was he looking so shell-shocked? What had shocked him? The way she'd given in, after refusing all those other times? The sight of her tears? The memory of those rash words she'd uttered? *I love you.* Mack would run a mile if he thought she wanted to put a permanent noose around his neck.

She half smiled at the irony of it. She was the one who ought to be running a mile—from *him.* Unless she was prepared to end up like her mother, tied to a man like her father.

And she wasn't prepared to! Never would she live

the kind of life her mother had had to endure. Her mother might have loved her husband to the end, but her love had been sorely tested, time and time again. It had barely survived.

Suzie struggled to sit up.

"Mack, I'd better—"

"Why didn't you tell me, Suzie?" His hands gripped her bare arms, making her acutely aware that she was still completely naked. And she didn't have the protection of the dark anymore. Worse—Mack was still naked, too! The sight of his raw masculinity clogged the breath in her throat. "Why didn't you tell me this was your first time?"

Suddenly shy, not wanting to look at him, not wanting him to look at her, she shook off his hand and reached for the tracksuit lying in a crumpled heap where he'd dropped it, wanting to cover her nakedness so that she could face Mack without being conscious every second of what had just happened. Because it must never happen again. With Mack there could be no rosy future, no happy ending.

"You never slept with Tristan Guthrie," Mack said wonderingly, his eyes bemused. "He was your fiancé, and today was to have been your wedding day, but you've never made love to him." He slanted a dark eyebrow. "You were saving yourself for your wedding night?"

Her eyelashes fluttered away. Was she? Was that why she'd never gone all the way with Tristan, and why her fiancé had never pressed her to? Because he'd wanted to wait, too? To make their wedding night special? As special as she'd imagined *he* was—until today?

But she knew it went deeper than that. Tristan's

kisses had never fired the passion in her that Mack's kisses always had. If Tristan's lips, his touch, or even a mere glance, had possessed half the impact of Mack's, she wouldn't have been *able* to resist him!

"I have to go...."

"Go? After—" He bit the rest off, his face darkening. "Just what did tonight mean to you, Suzie?" he growled. "Were you making love to me on the rebound, as a way of hitting back at Tristan? Were you imagining that *I* was Tristan, and that you were legally married to *him* in a marriage that was going to last? Was I just a convenient substitute like I was at the wedding?"

He caught her hand as it flashed toward his cheek. "Are you angry because I've hit on the truth, Suzie? Don't bother to answer. You've made it plain it's not *me* you want!"

She opened her mouth to deny it, to cry out that she did want him, that she'd always wanted him, never more than now. But her mother's plaintive warnings and the years of bitter turmoil were too deeply ingrained.

"I've just had one lucky escape. I'm not rushing headlong into another disaster!" She rolled away from him and scrambled to her feet. "Will you call me a cab, Mack? I want to go home." She would slip into her house the back way and go straight to bed.

"So it meant nothing to you." Mack's black eyes sought and impaled hers. "You could have fooled me, Suzie."

"It was only sex, Mack." *Only sex?* She quivered. *Only a heart and body and soul torn asunder!* "You should know all about that." Her eyes taunted him.

"You must have had plenty of women in your wild bachelor life."

"Not since I met you."

She gave a scathing laugh, disbelief in her eyes. "You haven't had sex for three years? I don't believe you!"

"I've sublimated my desire for you in other ways," he mocked. "By keeping myself busy."

"Oh, yes, doing what? Gazing into a computer? Bumming around Australia on your Harley-Davidson?" But she didn't really want to hear. She'd heard too many stories already about the hours he spent surfing the Internet, playing useless games and dreaming up hot new ideas that never came to anything...or idling round the countryside on his Harley.

She drew in her lips. Or did he mean he'd been keeping busy at the casino—winning and losing money, and no doubt getting more and more hooked each time?

Best not to know.

"Never mind," she mumbled, and gave a shrug—a valiant shrug. "Tonight was just one of those things." *One of those things that change a woman forever.* "We were caught up in the heat of the moment. It happens."

"Was that all it was, Suzie? Just a momentary lapse, in the heat of the moment?"

"Yes!" She tossed her curly head. "And you've no need to worry about any unwanted consequences...you're perfectly safe." This should be a safe period of the month for her. "Good night, Mack!"

Unable to face him a second longer, she stumbled away from him, taking care not to trip over anything on her way to the door. It would be so humiliating, if not downright dangerous, to land flat on that carpet again! "I'll wait out on the front porch for the taxi. Would you call for one *now?*"

"Suzie, you can't leave like this." As the taxi pulled up outside, Mack followed her down the steps. The rain had eased to a drizzle. "Promise you'll see me again. You can't deny there's something between us. We have something special."

Never had he sounded more compelling, more seductive, more persuasive.

"I know it's going to take time to get over Tristan, Suzie, if you truly *were* in love with him."

But I wasn't, she screamed silently. I know that now. I've only ever been in love with *you,* Mack—the last man in the world I'd ever want to get permanently tied up with, even if you were the family-man type. And I do still believe in marriage and happy families, believe it or not, even after all this. If only you were less like—

She snapped off the anguished thought. "Sometimes special feelings just aren't enough."

Mack caught her arm. "So it's another Tristan Guthrie you want." He scowled. "Money, success, an impeccable background. A man in a classy Italian suit, with film-star looks and quaint old-fashioned restraint when it comes to sex before marriage." His eyes, a dark glow in the wash of the streetlight, mocked her. "Or perhaps you'll take *him* back, once he has his divorce." A tiny flame smoldered in the black depths.

"I don't want *any* man right now—or in the foreseeable future!" she cried. "I just need to get away.

Right away, from everyone. From you, from Tristan, from my mother, from—from *Sydney.*''

She'd been doing some furious thinking as she'd been waiting for the taxi. An exclusive bridal boutique in Melbourne needed a new designer and the owner had offered her the job, with full artistic control over her designs—which she didn't always have working for Jolie, fun though it had been. And she wanted to specialize in bridal gowns; the accolades she'd received today had convinced her of that. One day, maybe, she would be rich and famous enough to have her own label.

''Winning the Gown of the Year award has opened doors for me,'' she said with a toss of her curls. ''And today's publicity should help, too. There's a great job down in Melbourne that I had to decline because I was marrying Tristan. But now...''

''You intend to go and live in *Melbourne?*'' Mack's dark eyes glinted with surprise. And frustration. He couldn't lose her again. Not *now!*

She wavered. ''Well...maybe.'' She wished she hadn't told Mack where she was thinking of going. She didn't want him following her to Melbourne, and weakening her resolve. Not that it would do him any good, because she wasn't going to change her mind about him, no matter how difficult it would be to cast him from her life now, after what had just happened.

But she mustn't let her feelings for Mack cloud her judgment. Agonizing as it was going to be to turn her back on him, it would be a thousand times more difficult to see the love she felt for him eroded over the years by soul-destroying debts, gambling, drinking and emotional turmoil.

No! Never! She was *not* going to live her mother's life all over again.

"I've had other offers from other states too," she said quickly. "I'll be considering all my options. My career," she stressed, "is going to come first from now on, and I don't want any man getting in my way." Her blue eyes flashed with a steely light, showing him she meant it. Trying to *convince* him—and herself!—that she meant it.

"If I hadn't intervened in your life," Mack reminded her, "I would never have discovered Tristan's shabby secret six weeks ago!" Desperation had loosened his tongue, making him blurt out the truth without thinking.

Suzie stopped. "*What* did you say? You knew *six weeks* ago that Tristan was already married?"

Mack cursed his unruly tongue. "I had to make sure. Check that he hadn't applied for a divorce. Damn it, Suzie, I never thought you'd go ahead with it. I kept hoping you wouldn't, even up to the very last minute. That you'd realize what a jerk he is and that you and I—"

"Were meant for each other?" she cut in scathingly. She frowned, her mind ticking over, fast and furious. "And just when, precisely, did *you* decide to marry me, Mack Chaney?" He'd told her he'd obtained special permission at the last minute, but how could that be? A month's notice was required, from memory. She'd been too dazed at the time to question it.

Mack grimaced. He'd expected her to be more grateful to him for coming to her rescue, not to concern herself with trivial details. "I filled out the form a month ago," he admitted, "on the off chance I could persuade you to marry *me* when you found out the truth about Tristan.'' A coaxing smile edged his lips. ''I never really dreamed…''

''You know why I married you, Mack,'' she stormed, ''and it had nothing to do with you!'' *Oh, no? Would she have allowed any other man to sweep her into marriage, even a short-lived marriage, at a moment's notice?* ''I can't believe that you've known for six *weeks* about Tristan's marriage and didn't tell me! Or that you gave notice of our marriage a *month* ago, and let me think it was a last-minute thing! You're as—as devious and underhanded as Tristan!''

''Hey, hang on, Suzie—''

But she was too incensed to listen. ''My mother always warned me never to trust you, Mack Chaney, and she was right! You and Tristan have proved to me that men are never to be relied on. I intend to make a success of my life, *on my own,* and I don't want you or Tristan or anyone else interfering!''

With each word her heart was breaking a little more, yet she meant every word she uttered. ''Good-bye, Mack,'' she said with the same iron resolve in her voice, but she couldn't look at him. He'd always had the power to weaken her, to change her mind and compel her to come back to him. If she gave in this time and agreed to see him again—to forgive him for what he'd done—she would be lost forever. She would never be able to give him up.

''Thanks for saving me from making a big mistake today.'' *Don't tempt me into making another.*

She ran to the cab without risking a final glance at him—much as she longed to—or waiting for a last word from him, enticing her to come back to him. She had to make Mack Chaney believe that this was the last time he would ever see her.

Because that was how it had to be.

Chapter Six

Melbourne

Suzie rocked her baby daughter in her arms and marveled, as she so often had in the past six months, at how lucky she was to have such a beautiful, healthy, happy baby.

Being a single mother hadn't been as difficult as she'd imagined. Priscilla, her boss at the bridal boutique where Suzie had been working since arriving in Melbourne sixteen months ago, had been wonderful and had supported her all the way. Luckily she'd kept well during her entire pregnancy, with no morning sickness at all, just tiredness in the early months and at the end, when she felt as big as a whale. The baby had been almost a month late.

Having her mother to stay for a few weeks after the birth had helped her to get back on her feet, and living above the bridal boutique made it easy to pop in and out of the shop. And she was able to sew in the apartment while her baby daughter slept or amused herself with her rattles and toys.

"Like to go for a walk, Katy?" she asked, and her daughter gurgled. "Yes, I thought so. We'll have to rug you up because it's a cold day outside. You'll need a warm jacket, a cozy blanket and a woolly bonnet to keep your head warm."

She moved over to a chest of drawers that she'd bought secondhand and pulled out a beautifully knitted matinee jacket and matching woolly bonnet. Her mother, having taken time off work for those few weeks, had knitted an entire baby layout for her granddaughter, for which Suzie was eternally grateful.

Ruth had been dismayed at first to hear about the baby, but had stood by her daughter. Suzie had told her mother in her seventh month, deciding it best to prepare Ruth before the actual birth so that it didn't come as such a shock.

Her mother had asked if the baby was Tristan's, and Suzie had tartly informed her that the father of her child was out of her life now and she didn't want him mentioned again.

Looking at Katy now, at six months, there could be little doubt who her father was. Her lovely big eyes, which had been a deep purple when her mother was here, were now a striking dark brown. And her practically bald head of a few months ago was now covered in luxuriant silky black hair. Even her smile was Mack's. It was incredible.

And disturbing.

She wondered if Mack would have wanted to be involved in Katy's life if he'd known he had a daughter. She felt guilty sometimes that she hadn't told him.

If he could only see Katy—see how much she looked like him—how could he resist her? Not that Mack would want the full-time responsibility of a child or a family, she reflected with a sigh, and *she* certainly wouldn't want him back in her life, trying to act the responsible parent when she knew it wouldn't last and would ultimately backfire on Katy and herself.

But even if he shunned any responsibility for Katy's day-to-day care, he might insist on regular access visits to his daughter. And how would she be able to bear seeing him on *those* occasions? It would be torture!

Especially if he wanted to resume where they'd left off.

She trembled, knowing what a look, a touch, a kiss from Mack could do to her. How would she be able to keep him at arm's length? And she would have to, for Katy's sake. She was going to make sure that her daughter had a secure, stable, carefree childhood and an equally secure, stable, carefree future, and the wrong man in their lives, as she'd learned from bitter experience, could wreak havoc and lead to disaster. She didn't intend to take the risk.

Grabbing her jacket, she carried her daughter down the stairs and lowered her into the pram. Katy was rubbing her eyes and was almost asleep already.

"Right, Katy, love, off we go." She pushed the pram through the doorway, out into the street.

And almost collided with Mack Chaney!

She couldn't believe her eyes. Mack, here in *Melbourne?* He'd come *looking* for her? It was like a bad dream. A scary, breath-stopping, gut-churning dream. She was unprepared for this. Totally unprepared!

"How did you find me?" she demanded, deciding

that attack was the safest way to deal with this breathtakingly unexpected development. "Did my mother tell you where I was?" No, surely Ruth wouldn't. Not Mack. Never.

His mouth curved in that special, heart-wrenching way that only Mack Chaney had. No...not only Mack. Katy had the same way of curving *her* lip when she wasn't quite smiling. And in full flight, her beautiful smile was the image of Mack's.

"Your mother and I don't share confidences," Mack reminded her dryly. "No, it's taken a while to find you. None of your friends would admit to knowing where you'd gone, and your workmates at Jolie Fashions appeared equally in the dark—though I find it hard to believe that the fashion grapevine hasn't kept them informed."

She felt a flush warm her cheeks. She'd asked her friends and ex-workmates at Jolie not to tell Tristan Guthrie or Mack Chaney where she'd gone, or where she was working—that she needed time alone.

She lifted her chin, trying not to let her eyes rake over Mack as they so badly wanted to. There was something different about him, but she hadn't yet worked out quite what. "I told you, I needed to get right away from everyone back home for a while."

"Including Tristan Guthrie?" His tone was derisive, his eyes darkly brooding. He'd seen the baby in the pram. "Don't tell me you've let him back into your life? That he's living and working here in Melbourne now?" A pulse twitched at his temple. "At least I know you haven't married him, even if he has his divorce. You've never sought a divorce from *me*."

He seized her left hand. "You're still wearing my ring."

She snatched back her hand, her skin feeling singed by his touch. "Only—only for appearances." *Liar,* she thought. She treasured Mack's ring. She could dream that it meant something, could pretend that the dream hadn't ended on her wedding day. Her gaze fluttered to his. Did he want it back? Was that why he'd come looking for her? "Here." She tried to pull it off. "I—I'm sorry I didn't return it before." A coldness was creeping over her heart. *Had he come to ask for a divorce?*

"I don't want it back." He spoke sharply, and she paused. "I'll never give it to anyone else. Keep it." A sardonic twist curved his lips. "I know how much you and your mother value appearances." His dark gaze flicked to the sleeping baby in the pram. *"Is the child Tristan's?"* he demanded.

Suzie gulped hard, several times. If she admitted that Tristan wasn't the father, Mack might guess the truth. Did she want him to? Or was it best kept hidden—at least for the time being? Best for Katy's future security—and her own peace of mind?

Would Mack *want* to know that he had a daughter? Or would he run a mile at the very idea of unplanned fatherhood and the threat of responsibility? Did *she* want to deny her child a father; even a father Katy would see only rarely, on access visits? Assuming Mack would want to see his child.

What would be best for her baby daughter? For *their* daughter?

Her heart caught in panic as she saw Mack staring down at the baby. Would he see the likeness to himself?

Luckily, Katy was still fast asleep and her big dark eyes were hidden behind her curling lashes. Her soft black hair was also safely hidden under her snug-fitting woolly bonnet. Wrapped up as she was in her bunny rug, with only part of her face visible, she could have been a robust three-month-old—or even a newborn baby to someone unfamiliar with babies—rather than a petite six-month-old.

"You actually believe I would have taken Tristan back after—after—" she nearly said, *after I'd been with you,* but she hastily changed it to, "after what he did to me?" She couldn't let Mack go on thinking Tristan was back in her life—it wouldn't be right. Hopefully, Mack would assume that she'd met someone else since arriving in Melbourne. At least it would buy her some time.

The black eyes narrowed, stabbing hers. "If you're not back with him, who *are* you involved with? I thought you were through with men, that you were going to concentrate on your career?" He frowned. "The child *is* yours?"

Suzie flicked her tongue over her lips. "Yes, she's mine." *And yours,* her heart cried. She knew she ought to deny that she was involved with anyone else, but if she did that, Mack might guess the truth.

She stifled a tremor. "I have a new life now, Mack, here in Melbourne, and it's given me Katy," she said, picking her words with care. It wasn't quite accurate—her *old* life in Sydney had given her Katy—but it was close enough to the truth. Her daughter had been *born* here in Melbourne. "Katy's father doesn't live with us," she told him, wanting to be as honest as she dared.

She took a deep breath. "Mack, I'm doing fine, if that's what you came here to find out. I'm fine and I'm happy."

Happy? *Was* she? She glanced down at her baby daughter and felt guilty that she would even have to ask such a question. Of course she was happy. Katy had brought her a happiness she'd never known.

"You realize you can't marry," Mack rasped. "You're still legally married to me."

"I have no intention of marrying anyone," she said shakily. "I told you that before I left Sydney."

"Yeah...well, I was relying on you to stick to that."

Her eyes snapped to his, her heart missing a beat. Several beats. "If you think I've been waiting for *you...*"

Mack glanced down at the sleeping baby, a wry half smile on his lips. "Obviously not."

She flushed, biting back the retort on her lips. *I've no need of a man in my life. Katy is all I need.* Safer, she decided, to let Mack wonder if there *was* another man still in the wings.

By now she'd realized why he looked different. His hair was shorter! Not short, but certainly shorter and less wild than it had ever been in the past. And not only that, he was wearing a brown suede jacket with a darker brown open-necked shirt, not his usual black leather gear.

Mack's gaze lifted, his dark eyes scanning her face. "You look tired, Suzie." He frowned. "And pale. Have you been getting enough sleep? Enough fresh air?"

"I'm just about to take my baby for a walk in the fresh air," she reminded him tartly. "And I'm just fine, thanks," she asserted, glancing down at Katy to avoid his brooding gaze. *Tired out, and run off my feet, but fine.*

"Well, I'm glad you're okay, Suzie." Whether he was glad she was *happy,* he didn't say. "So Tristan Guthrie is past history, as far as you're concerned?"

She flicked a look up at him. He still didn't believe her?

"Yes, Mack," she said evenly. "He's past history. He's out of my life for good," she stressed. *As you have to be,* she tried to tell him with her eyes. But the thought gave her no comfort or satisfaction whatsoever.

"Good. Tristan Guthrie was never the man for you." Contempt glinted in Mack's dark eyes.

"Well, now that you know I've made a new life for myself, Mack, you can go home again with a clear conscience," she said lightly—though her heart felt anything but light. It was breaking all over again, cracking into jagged pieces. She looked for the expected relief in his eyes that would confirm that she'd been wise not to tell him the truth about Katy.

But he scowled. If he was secretly relieved that the responsibility of a child hadn't fallen on his shoulders, he was hiding it amazingly well.

She swallowed hard. "You rode down from Sydney on your Harley?" she asked, more for something to say—something safe—than out of any particular interest. Not that she expected any other answer but, *Sure, what else?* Mack never went anywhere without his precious Harley-Davidson!

But he surprised her, his lip curving as he answered smoothly, "No, I flew down. I'm staying at an apartment in town. I caught a cab here from the city."

Her eyes widened. How could Mack afford expensive airfares and cabs and city apartments all of a sudden? A sick feeling coiled through her stomach.

"You've had a big win at the casino?" she asked teasingly, feigning a lightness she was far from feeling.

He gave a crooked smile. "No, nothing like that. But I have had some success with a new Internet software package I've developed. A Web editor, if you know anything about the Net."

"I don't." She didn't even own a computer, and didn't want to own one, even if she could afford it. People wasted too much time on their computers. Well, Mack Chaney did.

"How's it going?" she asked, hoping he wouldn't launch into a detailed description that would mean nothing to her. It was all gobbledygook, as far as she was concerned.

He didn't, simply telling her, "It's selling well—beyond my expectations."

"Congratulations." There was a faint dryness in her tone. High time he made some money from his damned computer, even if he'd only managed to earn enough so far to cover airfares, taxis and accommodation.

She heard a faint sound and inwardly panicked. Katy was stirring! If she opened those beautiful dark eyes...those eyes that were so like Mack's...

"Mack, I have to take Katy for a walk." She moved off, hoping the motion of the pram would settle the baby down again as it so often did. She glanced down anxiously, and saw Katy peacefully asleep again—thank heaven!

"I'll come with you," Mack said promptly. "You don't mind, do you?" He fell into step beside her.

"I don't suppose I can stop you." She kept her face impassive, but her heart had picked up a beat and her palms felt hot and clammy on the metal handle of the pram.

"You're not even a little bit pleased to see me?"

Her head jerked round, her eyes disbelieving. Even the existence of a baby—another man's baby, as far as Mack was aware—and a possible lover lurking in the wings, hadn't discouraged him?

It made her wonder nervously what he had in mind. Was he actually hoping to resume where they'd left off regardless of her baby or a possible lover?

The arrogance of the man! Typical Mack Chaney!

Or didn't he believe there *was* another man in her life? Was he sticking around simply to find out? And when he found out there wasn't...would he make his move then, hoping for another one-night stand with his legally wed wife, before he flew back to Sydney?

She quickened her steps. No way, she thought, her heart racing with the breath-stopping fantasies that swirled into her mind. She mustn't let it happen. She daren't get that close to him again.

Because another night in Mack's arms and she might never be able to let him go.

Her father's tormented face swam into her vision and she squeezed her eyes shut. No, she mustn't let it happen. Whatever it might cost her, she wasn't going to put Katy's future security at risk.

Chapter Seven

Mack caught up with her in a couple of long strides. "How's the fashion designing going?" he asked, not pressing her, thankfully, for an answer to his previous question. "Did your wedding day have the desired effect? *Our* wedding day," he corrected, his eyes glinting. "Did the publicity save Jolie Fashions? And help your own career as well?"

"Jolie's thriving again, thanks." That alone—and her beautiful daughter, of course—made the trauma of that highly emotional day worthwhile. "And my own career...well, it's a bit difficult with a baby. Katy comes first," she stressed. She'd happily thrown all her energy and money into making a secure life for her daughter, rather than seeking fame and fortune for herself.

"But Priscilla is wonderful to work with," she said warmly. "She lets me choose my own hours, and gives me total control over my designs. She's even offered me a partnership in her business."

"Well, that's big time." He sounded genuinely impressed. "Are you going to accept?"

"I can't afford it at the moment," she admitted. Any money left over from her daily living expenses she was putting aside for Katy's future. For her daughter's education and her security. "But I've been working long hours and saving madly." *In between feeding and tending to Katy and taking her for walks and going shopping and cleaning the flat.* "I work in the evenings as well as during the day, so you never know. Maybe one day."

It depended on whether her bank would give her a loan and if she could keep up the repayments. "Once I put Katy in day care, which I'll have to do when she starts walking and getting under my feet, I'll be able to work longer hours and see more clients."

"It sounds as if you're doing it pretty tough, Suzie."

She thought Mack was being sympathetic until he added with a hint of cynicism, "You've obviously had no luck as yet finding another well-heeled golden boy to take care of you?"

Her eyes flashed silvery sparks, hot anger mingling with a twinge of hurt. "I don't need *any* man to take care of me—rich or not. I'm managing perfectly well on my own." As soon as the words were out of her mouth she could have bitten off her tongue. Now Mack would know she had no man in her life. Damn!

She hastened to muddy the facts. "But just because I choose to live on my own doesn't mean I don't have a—a friend."

"Your baby's father?"

She glanced up at the harsh note in his voice, but the brooding dark eyes were unreadable. She drew in a deep steadying breath. "Yes. Katy's father is still around," she said carefully—in all honesty, "but I'd rather not talk about him, if you don't mind." It would be far too dangerous! "My private life is no longer any of your business, Mack."

"That was your choice, Suzie, not mine."

"Oh?" She knew she shouldn't pursue the subject, but she couldn't help it. "You're saying you would have wanted to settle down to a normal married life with a wife and children?" Her eyes mocked him. "I don't think so." Mack had never wanted a *normal* life—not the kind of life she wanted for her child. A settled, stable, secure life with a responsible father who earned a regular income, a man who would never fall into a black pit of despair and resort to addiction to blot out his pain and frustration.

"But it's what *I'd* like one day," she admitted, unable to hide a faint yearning in her voice, "especially now that I have a daughter. But only if the right man comes along," she stressed, knowing in her heart that there would only ever be one man for her. The wrong man!

"So Katy's father is not the right man?"

She gulped in a fractured breath. This double-talk—this cautious skating along the edge of the truth—was positively nightmarish!

"Unfortunately not," she answered, trying to keep her voice steady but unable to conceal a betraying tremor. "Even if he wanted to marry me, I wouldn't marry him. He...he's a bit like you, Mack," she said recklessly. "Not into responsibility or holding down a steady job or looking to the future."

She kept walking briskly as the words wrenched from her, her face turned into the unseasonably cold

September wind. "I want security and peace of mind for Katy, not the kind of life I had with *my* father."

"You say *unfortunately.*" Mack seized on the word. "I take it that means you still care about this man...irresponsible as he is?"

She hesitated, her heart skittering. This was hazardous territory. If he guessed she was talking about *him*...

"If I hadn't cared for him," she said huskily, "I would never have..." she was about to say "*had sex with him,*" but that would reduce the most wonderful experience of her life to a coldly clinical level, devoid of any real feeling. And there *had* been real feeling—on her part at least. "...made love to him," she concluded instead.

"You made love to me, too, once, Suzie," Mack reminded her. "Did you care for me, too...back then?"

Her heart swooped to her toes. She couldn't look at him. "Those were unusual circumstances," she hedged. "Please don't remind me of that traumatic day, Mack." As if she could ever forget it!

Oh, Mack, please go, before I throw myself back in your arms!

A sigh hissed through his teeth. "You obviously didn't take long to forget it and find someone else." There was a tinge of bitterness in his voice. "You must have met this other guy fairly soon after you arrived here in Melbourne, Suzie—to have his baby already."

The fine hairs rose at the nape of her neck. Was he beginning to suspect the truth already? Before he'd even seen Katy's dark eyes and black hair and the smile that was so like his?

"He reminded me of you, Mack." It was a desperate grab for a way out. "And you know how I could never resist *you.*"

He didn't like that. Glowering, he fell silent for a few minutes. She quickened her pace, wanting to get home before Katy woke up. She'd chosen to walk around the block of shops—she hadn't dared go any farther—and they were now approaching her apartment from the opposite direction. Not far to go now.

Please, Katy.

"You said you flew down to Melbourne, Mack. How come you didn't ride down on your Harley?" She hoped a return to his favorite topic might prove safer than perilous repartee about her mysterious lover. And talking about his Harley would be a salutary reminder of her father and *his* Harley and the glaring similarities between Mack and her irresponsible parent.

"I've sold it," Mack said coolly. "I've bought myself a car."

Her head whipped round. "You've sold your *Harley?*" She couldn't believe it. It must have been like ripping off his right arm.

Her father would never have parted with his beloved Harley in a million years. Even when he'd been deep in debt, he'd never considered parting with his precious motorbike. His Harley was his sole means of escape from his dark world, his one snatch at freedom in a life trapped by his gambling and his frustrations as an artist. His *gambling* had certainly provided no escape. It had been a shameful obsession, a fatal compulsion.

Her father's death had been put down to a genuine accident, triggered by alcohol, but Suzie had often wondered, painfully and in secret, if his beloved Harley had provided the ultimate escape for him.

"*Why* did you sell it?" she pressed Mack, without knowing why she would bother to ask or even care. "I thought you loved your Harley more than anything else in your life." As her father had.

"Not everything," Mack said. He wasn't looking at *her*—and why in heaven's name should he be? she asked herself fractiously—his brooding gaze turned inward as if he were reliving the harrowing moment of parting from his prized possession. What, she wondered, could he love more than his precious Harley? His new car? No doubt a flashy, open-topped sports car with Mag wheels and a souped-up motor.

Or was there something he loved even more? *A new woman in his life?*

Did he have a new woman in his life? She was shocked at the sharp stab of jealousy that knifed through her. *I'll never give it to anyone else,* he'd said about his wedding ring. But maybe he intended to buy a *new* one....

But he hadn't asked for a divorce.

"Mack, why are you here?" she snapped in frustration.

He turned to her then, his eyes faintly mocking. "I wanted to make sure you were all right, Suzie. Your mother wouldn't tell me where you were and your old friends didn't seem to know—or wouldn't tell me if they did—so I decided to methodically check out every fashion house and boutique in Melbourne until I struck the jackpot."

"How did you know I was in Melbourne?"

"You told me you'd been offered a job here, remember? Mentioning offers from other states was just a red herring, wasn't it?'' She couldn't meet his eyes.

''Yeah, of course it was. Still, if I hadn't found you in Melbourne, I would have tried Adelaide, then Perth, then Brisbane. I wouldn't have stopped, Suzie, until I found you.''

A tremor riffled through her. He'd been that desperate to find her? ''Well, I'm glad I didn't put you to all that trouble,'' she said lightly, trying to cover the chaotic emotions churning inside her. ''How many bridal boutiques,'' she asked curiously, ''did you check out before you struck the jackpot, as you put it?''

''Oh, once I started checking *bridal* boutiques, I was home and hosed. It seems you're quite famous already in the world of bridal design. When did you decide to specialize? After all that publicity on our wedding day?''

Our wedding day...how he loved to keep on reminding her!

She gulped, and shook her head. ''That only made up my mind for me. I'd already been toying with the idea before then. There's so much scope with bridal gowns these days.''

''Well, I'm glad you've found your niche, Suzie. By the way, your colleague Priscilla was most charming and helpful.''

Priscilla, Suzie mused, was always charming and helpful. Always hoping that her young designer—a single mother with a baby—would meet up with a man. Or decide to reunite with Katy's father—whoever he might be. Suzie had never confided in her boss to that extent. She had never dared. When she'd first arrived in Melbourne, she'd told Priscilla that her surprise wedding to Mack Chaney, which had featured in all the fashion magazines, had been a mistake, and that she'd left him after the ceremony. She hadn't mentioned his name since.

"Prissy didn't tell you I had a baby?" she asked carelessly.

"I didn't stop to chat. I only asked for your address. She said she wasn't at liberty to give it to me, but by sheer luck I ran into you as I left the boutique. You came out of the side door, so I gather you live on the premises."

Suzie's skin prickled. Had Priscilla recognized Mack from the wedding photographs circulating around the fashion world a year or so ago? He looked different now.

What had happened in the past sixteen months to bring about such a change in him? Well, it was a big change for Mack Chaney. Having a haircut. Giving up his beloved motorbike and his black leather gear. Buying a car. Whatever he'd earned so far from his new Internet Web editor must have gone to his head!

But at least he hadn't gambled his money away. She chewed on her lip. Maybe Mack wasn't so like her father after all.

Not *yet*, a cautionary voice warned. He mightn't be hooked *yet*. But if he kept earning money, and if he still liked gambling...

A sigh slipped from her lips. A gambler needed money to gamble. Mack—an honest man, as far as she knew—would never steal, borrow or cheat to get money. But if he'd *earned* it...if he'd found himself with an abundance of cash in his hands...

She flicked the distasteful thought away.

"Well, as you can see, Mack, I'm fine," she said

crisply. Or she meant to sound crisp, but there was a faint quaver in her voice.

"*Are* you, Suzie?" She could feel his eyes boring into her averted profile. "You're living away from home, you're trying to make a living on your own, with a new baby and no help, as far as I can see. How are you managing? *Really?*"

He sounded genuinely concerned, and she felt a swift pang, wishing for a mad moment that he'd been here in Melbourne to share the past sixteen months with her—or at least the past six. With her and Katy. His daughter.

She tried to make light of any difficulties she'd had. "My mother was here with me for the first few weeks. And I'm managing just fine—truly. I have a job I love, even though I've had to cut down my hours since I had the baby. But I'm determined to keep Katy at home with me for as long as possible—certainly until I stop nursing her." Which wouldn't be too long now. She was already supplementing Katy's feeds with the occasional bottle.

"I can see you're a devoted mother, Suzie." There was warmth in his voice, and it was playing havoc with her emotions. She'd longed to hear that warmth again, had dreamed of it at night, both in her waking moments and while asleep.

"I love Katy more than anything," she said passionately, and felt her heart wrench. She could have loved Mack as much if she'd dared to keep him in her life. If she'd dared to take the risk.

"Well, here we are." She paused as they reached the door of her apartment building, but she didn't look at Mack. She couldn't trust herself to, afraid she might show the apprehension she felt deep in her heart. Now that he'd found her and had satisfied himself that she was all right—*and that she hadn't changed her mind about him*—would he turn around and head straight back to Sydney? Would she never see him again?

"How long are you here in Melbourne, Mack?" she heard herself asking, still avoiding his eyes—that dark, compelling, bone-weakening gaze that was still as potent as it had ever been. She held her breath as she waited for his answer, longing in her heart to see more of him, but knowing, with the cold logic of her *head,* that it would be totally unwise. *Madness.*

"Oh, I intend to stay in Melbourne permanently," Mack informed her coolly, his eyes a dark glitter in the sharp afternoon sunlight, which had just pierced the heavy layer of cloud.

Shock flew through her. He was going to *stay* here?

"I've no longer a home or family ties back in Sydney," Mack said. "I sold the old family home when I sold my bike. The land was worth more than the house, which won't surprise you. The house will be pulled down and replaced with flats."

Suzie felt a momentary pang. Rude as she'd been at times about Mack's old home and its state of disrepair, it held memories of some happy times. Bittersweet memories.

"Still, the sale will help to finance new digs here in Melbourne," Mack said with satisfaction.

She glanced up at him, wanting but not daring to ask why he'd decided to move to Melbourne. She was struggling to come to grips with the fact that he was now living in the same city. After she'd fled Sydney to put distance between them!

It was on the tip of her tongue to ask for more

detail about his move, but she bit back the question. To ask would be showing too much interest in him. It might encourage him. Encourage him to come back to see her another day.

Or on some dark, seductive night.

She felt an upsurge of longing, and instantly quenched it. Or tried to. She mustn't weaken! She must think of Katy's future...her precious baby daughter's long-term security and happiness. She must remember her tormented father, and her mother's long years of struggle and despair. And her own troubled childhood, striving to understand the chaos around her. She had to be strong.

"Mack, I have to go." Katy was making faint sounds. Any second now she would open her eyes. And even though she'd told Mack that Katy's unnamed father reminded her of *him,* which would hopefully explain away the baby's dark eyes and hair, Mack might see other similarities that were specifically his. She'd seen them herself. Tiny gestures, expressions, smiles.

Mack moved a step closer to the pram and she drew in her breath.

"You said Katy's father reminded you of me, Suzie." He cocked an eyebrow. "Were you referring to our looks—or the fact that he's as irresponsible as you like to think I am?"

She dropped her gaze under the hard glitter of his. "A bit of both," she mumbled out. "He has dark eyes and black hair like you, Mack, and he—he's just as unsuited to marry and settle down."

She heard him heave in a deep, frustrated breath. "So you and your mother still think I'm as irresponsible as your father was. That I'm an unreliable misfit with no social graces, no respectable occupation and no solid prospects for the future.''

His harsh tone cut through her. ''Mack...'' Her voice trailed off. It was close enough to the truth, wasn't it?

''You should have tried looking beyond the black leather and the Harley, Suzie. You've never even attempted to see the real me. You've only seen what you've wanted to see.'' Mack's lip quirked, more in derision than humor. ''Your mother's made you paranoid.''

''You didn't live with my father!'' It was a ragged cry. What did he mean by *the real me?* She'd known the real Mack Chaney for years! She shouldn't listen to him. He was just trying to break down her defenses so that he could worm his way back into her life. *Or into her bed.*

''Look, I have to go in,'' she said, swinging away from him. ''Goodbye, Mack. Good luck with whatever you're doing in Melbourne.'' She fumbled for her key and unlocked the door opening onto the street.

Mack's hand closed over hers, and her heart stopped. And started again, racing wildly. His hands, his touch, had always had this tumultuous effect on her. This weakening effect. They were such beautiful hands, warm and strong, yet gentle, the kind of hands that made a woman feel loved and protected.

And if *that* wasn't madness! Protected? Mack Chaney would be the last man in the world a woman would rely on for protection!

''Do you still love him, Suzie?'' There was a grim urgency in his voice. ''Even if you're not living together, are you still seeing him?''

Still seeing her phantom lover? *Still seeing Katy's father?* She could feel her body trembling, her heart jumping. How could she think straight when he was holding her hand like this? When he was so close? She clawed her mind back.

"I don't *know* how I feel about him," she breathed hoarsely. Would she be dicing with disaster to see Mack again? "I—I shouldn't have anything more to do with him. I have to think of what's best for Katy." And for *me,* she thought in despair.

She broke away from him at last, opening the door into the lobby and hauling the pram through the doorway. Katy was awake and crying now, her tiny mouth opening and shutting in anguished squawks, her eyes squeezed shut, her sweet little face screwed up. If Mack had caught a glimpse of her like this, there was no way he would have seen any resemblance to himself!

"Goodbye, Mack." She tried to make it sound final. She needed breathing space. Time to think. Time to consider what would be best for Katy.

She heard Mack say something. It sounded like, "Good to see you, Suzie," but the words were lost under Katy's wails.

She blew out a sigh of relief as she shut the door after her, blotting Mack from her sight. He hadn't guessed. He hadn't suspected. She could rest more easily now.

But for how much longer?

She half expected, half dreaded a return visit from Mack the next morning, despite giving him scant encouragement to come back. When there was no sign of him, or the next day either, or for the remainder of the week, she found herself wishing, contrarily, that he *would* turn up, dangerous though she knew it would be if he did.

Once he saw Katy awake—

She puffed out a sigh. How could she go on denying Mack the chance to know his own daughter, now that he was living here in Melbourne? What right did she have to keep him in the dark any longer? She was his daughter as much as hers.

But she'd be mad not to find out more about Mack before telling him about his daughter. Was his new job, selling his Web editor over the Internet, going to last? Or would it fizzle out like all his other bright ideas and high-minded projects? Was he still gambling? Still drinking? Had he bought his new car with his own hard-earned cash, his own efforts, or from a big gambling win? It would only be by seeing more of Mack that she would find out.

But what if he didn't come back? Now that he'd seen her with a baby—presumably another man's child—he might have decided to bow out of her life for good this time.

Oh, Mack…Mack…

Having seen him again, and knowing that he was living here in Melbourne, made it doubly difficult to put him out of her mind. Despite the boundless joy her daughter brought her, and the sewing and designing and household chores that kept her busy day and evening, she found herself thinking of Mack constantly, losing interest in her food, finding little excitement in new designs for clients, growing more restless and melancholy with each hour and day that passed. Even Priscilla noticed.

"Suzie, what's wrong?" she asked finally, as they

shared a rare quiet moment in the boutique between fittings, while there was no one in the shop browsing among the racks of bridal gowns. "You've been nervy and distracted all week. Sometimes you don't even hear me when I toss a question at you. Even Mrs. Fenshaw asked me if there was anything wrong with you after her daughter's fitting this morning. You're usually so bright and chatty, she said."

Suzie flushed, summoning a contrite smile. The last thing she wanted was to lose her job. She was in no position to go it alone *yet.* Not by a long way. "Sorry, Prissy, I guess I've been burning the candle a bit too much the last few days. And Katy's teething and hasn't been sleeping well at night. I'll apologize to Mrs. Fenshaw."

"Oh, she can take it." Priscilla dismissed Mrs. Fenshaw. She was more concerned about her young designer. "It's that guy you met outside the boutique last week, isn't it?" she asked directly. She'd seen them through the window. "Suzie, I know you don't want to talk about him...."

Priscilla had been all agog the next morning to know who he was and to hear all about him. If she'd recognized Mack from their wedding photographs, she hadn't let on.

Suzie had fobbed her off with a careless, "Oh, he's just someone I used to know back home. I doubt if I'll be seeing him again. I didn't exactly encourage him to stick around." And she'd turned away with a firmness that showed that she wanted no further questions about him.

"Prissy, there's no point talking about him," she said now, with a sigh. "There's nothing to tell."

"Isn't there?" Priscilla slipped an arm round her

shoulder. ''Sometimes it helps to talk to someone. I'm a good listener, Suzie. And I can keep my mouth shut. You know how much gossip we hear every day from our darling clients and I never repeat any of it.''

Suzie shook her head helplessly. How *could* she tell her? She hadn't even told Mack that he was Katy's father. It wouldn't be right to tell anyone else—not even Prissy—while Mack was still in the dark.

''He was very good-looking,'' Priscilla mused aloud. ''In a dark, brooding, interesting sort of way. The kind of sexy hunk that any red-blooded woman would fall for.''

Suzie's brow shot up. She hoped Prissy wouldn't notice the sudden heat in her cheeks. ''I wouldn't have thought he was your type,'' she quipped.

Priscilla laughed. ''He's the type who'd bowl over any woman. There's passion and energy and a capacity for powerful emotion simmering under those rugged good looks and mesmerizing black eyes. It radiates from him.''

Suzie looked startled. For Priscilla, a respectable, happily married woman to have noticed so much about a man who wasn't her husband... But it was only a *surface* judgment. Prissy had only seen him for a few minutes.

''Oh, Prissy, you don't even know him. He's—'' she hesitated, biting her lip.

''A bit wild? A bit wicked?'' Prissy grinned. ''We women love to go for the bad-boy type, don't we? Bad boys are more romantic and interesting. And so deliciously challenging. You always think you'll be the one to convert them. Harry was like that until I tamed him.''

"He *was?*" Diverted for a second, Suzie tried to picture the steady, smiling-eyed Harry as a bad boy, but she couldn't. He was such a responsible, successful businessman now, and very much the contented family man. His two young sons adored him. She'd been invited to their home a few times, and Harry was like a big kid himself when he'd fooled around with his boys.

"I've no intention of trying to convert Mack Chaney," she growled, compressing her lips at the thought of the long years her mother had spent trying to convert Suzie's father into a responsible, reliable, clean-living husband. It would be a losing battle all over again!

"Mack Chaney…ah!" As Priscilla pounced on the name, Suzie could have bitten off her tongue. The name had just slipped out. "So it *was* him. He looked different in your wedding photographs. And he was wearing black leather then. It was *so* romantic. Fancy him turning up here!"

Prissy looked at her expectantly, and Suzie panicked. What could she say? She didn't have the answers herself!

"Prissy, I'd better check on Katy." She'd left the baby asleep in her pram in the small room at the rear of the shop. "I want to make sure she's—" Her head snapped round as the outer door of the boutique jangled. But it wasn't a tall, black-haired ex-biker who walked in. It was a mother and daughter who'd come to look at bridal gowns.

Her stomach settled back into place. "Looks like you have some customers, Prissy," she whispered, and scuttled off, her pulses still racing with the release of nervous tension.

Chapter Eight

Another night and another morning passed without a word or a sign of Mack. Suzie wondered if he was doing it deliberately to whet her appetite for him.

Ha! she thought in scorn, though a more honest part of her knew that his ploy, deliberate or not, was working. She longed to see him again. Ached to see him. Ached to feel his arms around her, his sexy body crushing hers…

She'd dreamed of him last night and woken with her body on fire, throbbing with her need for him. But that was the very reason she had to keep him at arm's length. She had to listen to the logic of her *mind,* not the physical yearnings of her body.

She shut her eyes. She mustn't torture herself like this. She mustn't even think about him. She should be thinking about little Katy. The poor little mite had a sniffle and had been fretful all day, showing little interest in her food. Her tooth had already come through, so it couldn't be that.

Suzie had planned to do some sewing and designing upstairs during the afternoon, between feeds and tending to Katy, and to do more sewing in the evening after she'd put the baby down for the night, but she ended up doing no work at all.

Katy wouldn't settle down. She had no interest in her toys, or even in her bath, which she normally loved. She just wanted Suzie to hold her. To begin with she was simply a bit snuffly and out of sorts, but by early evening she was whimpering and burning up with fever.

Suzie called the local doctor's surgery, hoping they would be able to send a doctor, but being after hours, and a Saturday, there was only one doctor on duty, and he asked her to bring the baby to the surgery.

She was about to call a taxi, having no car in Melbourne, when she heard the buzz of her security intercom. She answered, asking rather sharply, because she was worried about Katy and anxious to get her to a doctor, ''Yes? Who's there?''

''Suzie, it's me, Mack. Look, I know you're probably busy—''

''Oh, Mack!'' She didn't know whether it was relief she felt, or annoyance. She only knew that his voice was doing crazy things to her heartbeat, and that she had more important things to think about right now than Mack Chaney. ''Mack, I can't see you now, my baby's sick and I need to call a cab and take her to the doctor.'' It came out in a rush.

''I'll take you,'' Mack said promptly. ''I brought my car tonight.''

''Oh, Mack, *would* you?'' It would save valuable time. Katy wasn't looking good at all. She was very pale and was just lying in her arms, barely moving.

''Katy's fever seems to be getting worse,'' she told him worriedly. ''And she's been vomiting.''

That would have been enough to put most men off—she couldn't imagine Tristan, with his immaculately kept, top-of-the-range Mercedes, allowing a vomiting baby onboard—but Mack merely said, ''Come on down now, if you're ready. Need any help?''

''I can manage, thanks.'' She didn't even pause to grab a jacket. She snatched up her purse and Katy's bag of diapers and other baby paraphernalia that went everywhere with her, and with the baby in her arms, flung herself out the door and down the stairs.

Mack had come back. After a week with no word from him, he'd come back, cool as you please.

Why would he come to see her so late in the day? *To see if she had another man with her?* Her heart quivered. Not just her heart. She realized she was trembling all over. With exasperation, she told herself. How dare he check up on her!

Mack was waiting outside. He was wearing his black leather jacket, just like the Mack Chaney of old, bringing back disturbing memories she couldn't think about now.

Darkness had fallen, with a blanket of cloud hiding the moon and the stars. But the streetlights were on and she could see several cars parked along the kerb. There was no flashy open-topped sports car that she could see. But, realistically, how would Mack Chaney be able to afford an expensive sports car? She'd been mad to imagine that he could—much as he might have loved to own one.

She was dying to ask what he'd been doing for the

past week, but wild horses wouldn't have dragged the question from her.

"This way," Mack said, and she glanced up the street, saw an old-model sedan with worn paintwork and dents on the side, and thought, *Yes, that'll be more like it.* But she didn't care how shabby or dented his car was as long as it had wheels and an engine.

He steered her past the old bomb to a shiny, modern sedan farther along. A respectable car, with a roof and four doors—and not a single dent that she could see. She couldn't believe her eyes.

"*This is your new car?*" she asked as he helped her in with the baby. Mack had no baby seat in the car, of course, so she had to cradle Katy in her arms.

"Yes...don't you like it?" he asked as he made sure she was buckled in securely.

"Well, yes, *I* like it—but then I like normal cars. I'm just surprised that *you've* chosen such a normal car."

He gave her a mocking glance, which changed instantly to concern as he saw her look down at Katy with a stricken expression.

"Oh, Mack, I'm so worried about her. She's gone all limp and floppy." This was no normal fever—the kind of fever young babies could get so easily. This was a *dangerously* high fever which could indicate something very serious. "She's really sick!"

"Forget your doctor, I'll take you to the hospital." Mack hurried round to the driver's side. "Straight to the Children's, I reckon."

She didn't argue with him. If Mack hadn't arrived when he had, she would have called an ambulance by now, even if she'd already phoned for a cab. Katy was going downhill fast, and Suzie was terrified.

"Thanks, Mack," she said gratefully as the engine purred smoothly to life and the car shot forward, as fast as safety would allow.

Thank heaven he has a decent car, Suzie thought. It was a very smooth ride—a very smooth car.

"What kind of car is this?" she asked, not really caring, but needing to say something. Anything.

"A BMW"

She blinked. Mack owned a *BMW?*

"You haven't robbed a bank or something, have you?" she quipped, but she wasn't really in the mood for jokes. And besides, he was more likely to have bought it with the profits of a big win at the casino—assuming he was a luckier gambler than her father. He'd been lucky that other time, with his huge win. Big, unexpected wins were just the way to get hooked, she thought with a dip of her spirits. It was the way her father had become hooked.

She fell silent after that, until they arrived at the hospital. Mack drove up to the emergency entrance, and she ran in ahead of him, with Katy in her arms. Just as she stumbled to the triage desk, Katy started fitting.

It was terrifying. Doctors and nurses came running, and rushed her to a nearby cubicle. Fortunately one of the doctors was the senior physician on duty, and he immediately took charge.

The next few hours passed in a frightening blur. It was worse, far worse than Suzie's worst nightmare. Her baby daughter, the doctor solemnly told her, had bacterial meningitis. If she and Mack hadn't rushed her to the hospital when they did, and if the baby hadn't been so promptly diagnosed and immediately put onto lifesaving intravenous antibiotics, Katy could have died.

As it was, she was still in grave danger, and would continue to be, the doctor warned her, for the next twenty-four hours. Babies and old people, he said, were the most vulnerable.

All they could do was wait.

And Mack, to her surprise, and secret relief, waited with her, refusing to leave her side. While little Katy lay as still and white as death, attached to lifesaving tubes, she and Mack sat by her cot in the isolation ward, watching worriedly over her.

''Thank God I came back when I did,'' Mack said roughly.

Suzie's head shot up. ''You've been away? You had to go back to Sydney?'' Had there been some hitch with the sale of his house?

''No, not to Sydney. I've been overseas.''

She blinked. Mack could afford an overseas trip? She felt a twinge that could only have been jealousy. Had he gone alone? ''Where to?'' she asked, thinking he'd say New Zealand or Fiji or Singapore—popular destinations for Australians wanting a reasonably cheap trip.

''Las Vegas.''

Las Vegas! Her jaw dropped, her heart plunging to her toes. *The gambling capital of the world!* ''Why would you want to go there?'' she asked hoarsely. *To gamble! Why else?*

''There was a computer convention there.''

Her eyes narrowed, searching his face. Was that true? How could Mack afford a trip to America? To an expensive place like Las Vegas!

He read the questions in her eyes. The doubt. ''I

was asked to give a talk on my new Web editor. A computer company sponsored me.''

''Oh.'' So the trip would have cost him nothing. And he'd gone there to *work.* Relief quivered through her. Mack was right, she thought with a tremor. Her mother had made her paranoid. ''How did your talk go?'' she asked, injecting warmth into her voice. She wanted to believe in Mack. She wanted it more than anything.

''Fine.'' He didn't go into details. Thinking, no doubt, that she wouldn't have understood if he had.

''I guess you played the tables while you were there?'' she heard herself asking with feigned lightness. *Tell me you're not a gambler, Mack. Make me believe it.*

''I wasn't there to play, I was there to work.''

''But you must have had free evenings.''

''I spent the evenings making contacts and socializing. You know how we computer nerds love talking about the Internet, and discussing ways of revolutionizing it.''

No, she didn't know what computer nerds liked to talk about. She only knew that gamblers liked to gamble. ''So you had no fun at all.''

''I wouldn't say that. But there wasn't a lot of time for fun and games. We only had three days there. The rest was traveling time. We did it pretty tough.''

''Well, you must be tired out.'' She kept any sarcasm from her voice, not wanting to condemn him on a vague suspicion.

Mack breathed in deeply, arching his back. ''Mm...I still feel a bit jet-lagged,'' he admitted. ''I haven't caught up on all the sleep I lost yet.''

Suzie felt her heart wobble. Was it only jet lag he

was suffering from? Or lack of sleep after three torrid nights—*all-night sessions*—in Las Vegas? A hardened gambler would find a way to gamble, even if he was tied up day and evening. Mack could have played the tables all night long!

"Well, why don't you go home and have a sleep now then?" she suggested without looking at him. "I'll be here to watch over Katy."

But he shook his head. "I can sleep later."

"Well, just say if you want to go."

I don't, Suzie...I'm just where I want to be, Mack thought, drinking in the tumbled honey-tinged curls, the oversize sweater concealing the soft curves he longed to run his hands over, the wary eyes that couldn't quite meet his—hell, he'd do anything to remove that wariness from them.

Almost anything.

He grimaced. There was one thing he wasn't going to be tempted to do, no matter how easy it would be to succumb, or how badly he longed to have her back in his arms where she belonged. He wasn't going to blow it this time. They had plenty of time. All the time in the world.

At least...

He clenched his teeth, then shrugged. If little Katy's father—an unreliable type, from what Suzie had let drop—*was* still around, and if he *did* still occupy a small corner of her heart, he was nowhere around now. He hadn't been at her flat earlier this evening, and she hadn't called him for help with Katy, or even since arriving at the hospital. And—Mack felt a tinge of satisfaction at the thought—Suzie didn't have the look of a woman who'd been with a man recently.

He knew what Suzie looked like after she'd been with a man, and the memory had been torturing him for the past sixteen months. He couldn't believe how patient he'd been, how focused he'd forced himself to be on other things than Suzie. But it would all be worth it if he won her back for good.

He had to! He couldn't face another rejection from her.

Suzie, glancing up at him, flushed under his brooding scrutiny. If he was going to look at her like that, letting him stay here with her mightn't have been a good idea.

She tugged her gaze away, relieved when a nurse came in to tell them they'd both have to have an injection.

"It's important to inoculate household members who've been in close contact with the disease."

Household members...close contact... The nurse was including Mack, of course. Suzie wondered if he would stay...or run. Tristan would have run for his life—he'd been scared to death of injections.

Mack stayed. He didn't argue about being inoculated. After all, his eyes told Suzie, he *had* been in contact with Katy, even if only briefly.

She gave him a quick smile as they followed the nurse out.

"Mack, you really don't have to stay," she said again later, when they were back in the isolation ward. "It could be hours before we know if—if—" She couldn't say it.

He slipped an arm round her shoulders. Never had an arm felt so strong, or so warm, or so comforting. She felt tears welling in her eyes, the tears she hadn't been able to shed over the past traumatic hours. She'd felt too numb, too terrified to cry. She still felt terrified, but Mack's strength was having its usual weakening effect. She wanted to lean into him and give way to her fears and let the tears flow. But she blinked and forced them back.

"You need someone with you." There was something in Mack's voice that made her glance up at him. His dark eyes were sympathetic, but any other expression was carefully masked. Was he wondering why Katy's father wasn't here with her? Wondering why she hadn't called him, and given him the chance to rush in from wherever he was to stand vigil over his daughter?

She felt a strangling sensation in her throat. Guilt rose like a tide. Her baby might die. *Mack*'s baby might die, and she hadn't even told him that Katy was his daughter!

"Mack." She had to tell him. Regardless of the consequences, he had a right to know. But—she glanced around—there were always nurses within earshot and doctors popping in and out. How could she tell him in front of strangers?

"Mack, I—I'd like to walk for a bit. Just along the corridor." Not too far from her baby. Not out of sight, if the doctors needed to find her. Just somewhere they could be alone for a few minutes.

But before they could leave, Dr. Curzon, the doctor who'd first diagnosed Katy's condition, strode in and bent over the baby's cot. He frowned in concentration as he examined Katy. Suzie held her breath, stark terror stopping her heart completely.

He eventually straightened. "No change," he reported solemnly. "But she's no worse," he assured her with a rallying smile.

Suzie was too worried to offer a smile in return. "How could she have caught this disease?" she burst out, twisting her hands in despair. "She's only a baby."

"It's more likely to hit children and babies, unfortunately, though Katy is very young to have it. It's transmitted by saliva," he told her. "Someone kissing the baby, perhaps, or coughing on the baby..." He was already backing away, other patients needing him. "I'll be back shortly." A quick smile and he was gone.

Suzie slumped deeper into her chair, huddling into her wooly sweater. She thought of all the clients at the boutique who'd fussed over Katy, who'd cuddled her, kissed her, breathed their germs over her. She shouldn't have allowed it!

But then Katy could have been exposed to germs at the supermarket, or at the health center, or anywhere.

"Come on, let's go for that walk," Mack said, and she sucked in a deep breath and nodded.

Out in the corridor she pulled him into a quiet corner and gripped his arm.

"Mack, there's something you have to know. About Katy."

She knew, the second the words were out—by the stiffening of his muscled arm under her fingers and the sudden dark gleam in his eyes—that Mack had instantly guessed the truth. He was no fool.

But he still wasn't sure. She saw the changing expressions in his eyes, but he veiled them quickly. He wasn't going to react until he'd heard the words from her own lips. After all, she'd mentioned another man. A man she still cared for. A man who reminded her of *him!* She could have decided she wanted him back, irresponsible as he was, because *he,* not Mack, was Katy's father.

Was that what he was thinking?

She didn't keep him in suspense. She wouldn't be so cruel.

"Katy's your daughter, Mack."

He didn't move, didn't react for a second, but his very stillness tangled the breath in her throat. Was he angry? Was he pleased? Was he furiously thinking of a way to get out of this...this *net* he'd been plunged into? The feeling of being trapped in a situation he'd never wanted, or expected?

Then his lips parted. Cold lips. His dark eyes were skeptical. "You said there was another man."

"I was talking about *you,* Mack!" she cried, and glanced round, hoping the sisters at the nursing station nearby couldn't hear. She was beginning to wish she'd kept her mouth shut until later—until Katy was out of danger—because now she had to turn her thoughts to Mack and what this was going to mean to *him,* when all she wanted to do was think of poor Katy, who was battling for her precious, fragile life.

What if Katy lost her battle?

Tears sprang to her eyes and threatened to spill over. Her baby daughter was so tiny...so frail...so vulnerable. And this was a terrible disease. She'd read of children who'd lost fingers or even died from bacterial meningitis. A deep shudder shook her. Why hadn't she considered that it might have been something like this, and brought Katy into the hospital sooner?

Thank heaven Mack had turned up when he had!

She hung her head, fighting back her tears, tears she knew she would never be able to stop if she let them come. If she lost Katy…

A moan slid from her lips. "Oh, Mack, I'm so frightened!" The cry was wrenched from her. "Katy could still *die.*"

She felt Mack flinch, and realized, with a surge of shame and understanding, how Katy's perilous state must be making *Mack* feel, now that he knew the truth. He'd never seen his daughter awake, looking up at him, smiling at him and chuckling at the sight of him.

Now he might never have that chance.

"Oh, Mack, I'm sorry!" The cry wrenched from her. "I—I didn't know what to do. Whether to tell you, what you'd feel about it, or—or if you'd even *want* to know!"

There was still no softening in his face, still no hint or word of how he felt, though the glitter in his dark eyes seemed…seemed…

She felt a rush of compassion. Was Mack holding back his emotion because he was afraid of *showing* any, or showing too much? Or afraid of *feeling* too much? He'd just found out that Katy was his daughter, and his baby might not survive the night!

"I'm glad you're here with me, Mack," she said impulsively, wanting him to know that they both shared this fear and anxiety together, that they were both here for each other, whatever happened between them in the future. "I—I've never needed you so much."

His hand came up to cover hers. Without saying a word, without spelling out what he felt or wanted to do in the future, he was letting her know that he was there for her. For now. For tonight.

For as long as their baby daughter was in danger.

For as long as they both needed him.

Mack wasn't sure what he felt. A whole gamut of emotions were chasing around inside him, shock, anger, elation, fear, disbelief, despair. *His* child. Not Tristan's, not some other man's, some irresponsible no-hoper who reminded Suzie of him. Katy was *his* child. His and Suzie's.

An overwhelming rush of feeling for the child they'd made together swooped through him, threatening his self-control. He brutally quenched it. Now wasn't the time to weaken and go soppy. Safer for the time being to let his anger ride uppermost.

"So." He turned dark, unreadable eyes to hers. "If I hadn't come to see you when I did, my daughter could have lived and died without me ever knowing she existed."

Suzie gave a choking cry. "Oh, Mack, don't even think such a— She mustn't die!" she cried brokenly. "She c-can't!"

Her anguish brought a betraying flicker to his eyes. "Katy won't die, Suzie. She's in the best of hands. You heard Dr. Curzon. She's holding her own. There's been no deterioration. That's a good sign, Suzie."

She looked up at him through a veil of unshed tears, his own anguish penetrating hers. "If I—if I'd known you would feel like this about her, Mack. That you would *want* to know her..."

His face darkened, his eyes scathing now. "You honestly imagined I wouldn't?"

She gulped, and shook her head. "I—I wasn't sure. I thought it would be best for Katy if—if— Damn it, Mack, I didn't want her to have the kind of life I had!" *The emotional ups and downs, the fights, the despair, the constant feeling of insecurity, the struggles to pay off unnecessary debts.* "I want her to have a secure, stable, carefree life."

"And you thought I wouldn't give her that?"

His tone was so grim that her eyes wavered. "Well *would* you? Would you even *want* to? You've never exactly struck me as being the settling-down type. The responsible family-man type, with a regular job and a regular income."

His brow plunged lower. "So you still think I'm like your father? That I'm incapable of holding down a proper job? That I'll bum my way through life and drink away any money I make?"

"Or *gamble* it away!" The fears she'd long harbored leapt out, her worry over Katy affecting her judgment, causing her to throw caution to the winds.

His eyes impaled hers, and she flinched. "You think—" He stopped, flicking his shoulder impatiently. "Don't let's fight, Suzie," he said wearily. "I'd like to see my daughter. Now that I know she *is* my daughter."

"Yes, yes, of course," Suzie said huskily.

Mack led the way, entering the isolation ward ahead of her. A nurse was there, but she melted away as he approached the baby's cot, his muscular body sending out powerful vibes that dared anyone to try keeping him away.

Suzie realized she was trembling. Partly in relief, because she'd finally unburdened her guilty secret, and partly at the thought of Mack seeing his daughter *as her father* for the first time.

What would his reaction be? Mack was so good at hiding his real feelings. But to have finally discovered that he had a daughter—that *Katy* was his daughter—and to realize at the same time that he'd nearly lost her. It must have shaken him. It *had* shaken him, she'd seen it in his eyes. It had made him angry, too, to know that she'd kept his daughter's existence from him.

But would he want to be involved in Katy's life, once his daughter was well again and he'd had time to let it all sink in? Would she *want* him to be? And what would it do to *her* if he did insist on staying around—or at least on having regular access to Katy?

She looked for a clue in his face as he bent over the hospital cot. The baby, with those scary-looking tubes still connected to her, lay as deathly still as before, too sick and weak to move or even to open her eyes.

She saw a visible change in Mack's expression as he looked down at his tiny, fragile, yet blessedly strong daughter, courageously holding her own—a real fighter, obviously. Katy's big dark eyes were, of course, hidden from him, but her fine black hair, so different from her mother's honey-kissed tumble of curls, was on full show.

"She's beautiful," Mack murmured, seeing Katy for the first time with a father's eyes. He reached down to touch his daughter's soft cheek with the tip of his finger. "She's just perfect."

His voice was hoarse and unsteady. And his eyes gleamed in a way Suzie had never seen before. Anybody watching would know that he was deeply moved. Whether the nurse standing by would guess that he had just learned that he was Katy's father... Well, what did it matter? All that mattered was that Mack was connecting with Katy, bonding with his child.

She felt tears squeezing from her eyes. She'd been afraid of what it might mean, not just to Katy, but to herself as well, if Mack came back into their lives. But seeing him with his baby daughter now, seeing the raw emotion in his eyes, she knew that this was right, and that she would never again do anything to keep Mack from Katy—whatever it might do to her.

Chapter Nine

The hours crawled by. Suzie and Mack sat up all that night and all the next day—it was a Sunday, luckily, so Suzie had no worry about clients needing fittings. She thought of calling Priscilla, but decided against it until Katy was safely past the critical twenty-four hour period.

If her baby did get safely past.

She shuddered, and Mack noticed and slipped a comforting arm round her.

From time to time sandwiches, coffee and snacks appeared, and they were offered beds if they wished, but both declined, insisting on sitting up to watch over Katy. Occasionally they dozed off where they sat.

As night fell—the second night of their long vigil—a nurse suggested they go down to the cafeteria for a proper meal and to stretch their legs. "I'll call you the moment there's any change," she promised. *Any change…for good or ill, she meant.*

Suzie was about to shake her head, but Mack insisted, pulling her to her feet. "You need a break. Come on, we won't need to be long."

Neither felt like eating much, but it was a change of scene, and the exercise—they used the stairs rather than the lift—helped to ease their stiff muscles.

They came back to the isolation ward to find a group of doctors and nurses bent over Katy's cot. Suzie stopped breathing, her heart seizing in panic. *Oh, God, please don't let Katy be any worse. Please don't let her die. Please, please, please let her get better.* She sensed that Mack, still and silent beside her, was holding his breath, too.

After a few minutes, one of the doctors came over to them—smiling. He was a new doctor, Dr. Curzon having already left for the night.

"Well, you can relax, the news is good," he told them, without dragging out the suspense. "Your daughter has passed the critical stage and is showing good signs of improvement." He smiled. "Her temperature is normal and she's picked up noticeably. She's even feeding. I'd say she looks set to make a full recovery."

"Oh, thank you, Doctor, thank you!" Suzie's grateful eyes were on the doctor, but she was clinging to Mack. His own hands were digging into her arms just as fiercely.

"It was lucky you brought her in so promptly," the doctor commended her. "If you'd delayed, thinking she was merely suffering an upper respiratory infection, it might have been too late to save her...or could have led to serious, permanent complications."

Suzie shivered. "You're saying Katy's going to suffer no aftereffects?" She raised pleading eyes to his, anxious to be reassured. She'd heard alarming stories of children who'd never fully recovered from the effects of this shocking disease.

"Well, we'll need to keep her in hospital for a couple of weeks. She'll have to keep on with the IV antibiotic therapy for a while longer, and we'll want to keep her under close observation. You can spend as much time with her as you wish," he assured her. "Perhaps the two of you could take it in turns to come in during the day, if you need to go to work or have other children to look after. It will help your daughter to see a familiar face when she's awake during the day."

Suzie felt Mack tense as the doctor uttered the words *familiar face,* and a prickly flush heated her cheeks. Did it hurt Mack to know that he wasn't a familiar face to Katy? Was he still angry that she'd kept him in the dark until now? Or was he already beginning to feel a little trapped? *Perhaps the two of you can take turns to come in....* Would he *want* to? Not just for the next day or two, but for a couple of weeks?

She shook off the questions she longed to ask. Katy was the only one she wanted to think about right now. "Can we see her now?" she asked, and the doctor nodded, and waved a hand for them to go ahead.

"By all means. Go and see your plucky little daughter."

It was after midnight on that long, seemingly endless Sunday that Mack finally dropped her home. Without her realizing it, her head had lolled onto his shoulder during the drive home, but as he pulled up outside her apartment building she forced her eyes open and tried to raise her head—swallowing as she realized she was leaning against Mack's shoulder.

"Oh, sorry, Mack. I must have dropped off." As she sat upright, a pain shot through her head. She felt like death! Reaction—the long, traumatic hours of waiting in fear, the ultimate relief, the lack of sleep—had finally caught up with her.

"You must get to bed," Mack said as he unbuckled his seat belt and helped to release hers. "You heard what the sister said. It's important you get your sleep. Katy's going to be fine, and you're not to go back to the hospital until you've had a good long sleep." He knew she would want to go back as quickly as possible. "You're to sleep until late tomorrow morning at the very least," he said firmly.

He insisted on seeing her inside—not just into the downstairs lobby, but up the stairs and into her flat. "I don't trust you not to fall asleep on the stairs—or in a chair," he murmured. "I want to make sure you go to bed—and stay there."

"But I—I can't go to bed yet," she protested. "I have appointments in the morning. I'll have to let Priscilla know that—"

"She'll be asleep now. I'll let Priscilla know first thing in the morning. She can cancel or postpone any appointments you have for the next few days. If any are absolutely vital, you can let me know what time they are and I'll make sure I'm at the hospital to cover those times. We'll do what the doctor suggested and take it in turns to go in and sit with Katy. That'll give you a chance to see clients or do some sewing during the day."

She raised heavy-lidded eyes to his. "But don't you have work commitments now?" She eyed him blearily. "You said you're selling this new Web editor of yours over the Internet. Doesn't that keep you busy during the day?" *When he wasn't flitting off to Las Vegas.*

"I can do that anytime, I'm my own boss." His lip quirked in a wry smile. "I can take time off when I want."

She stifled a sigh. Of course he could. He'd only work when *he* wanted to work. That was Mack all over. But she wasn't going to question it or argue with him—not now. "There's nothing I can't put off for a few days," she said after a moment's thought, "but if you're serious about wanting to sit with Katy for part of the day, I could catch up on some sewing while you're with her."

"Oh, I'm serious," Mack said, and the grimness was back in his voice. "I want to get to know my daughter, and I want her to get to know me. But I think the first couple of times she sees me, you should be with me." The black eyes held a challenging glitter. "Best to let her get used to me with you there, too, in the beginning."

The two parents together putting on a united front. Suzie swallowed hard. How long would it last, this togetherness? How long would Mack's eagerness to sit with a sick baby last? And was it wise to pretend to be a couple when they weren't?

Of course it was wise, if it helped Katy to know her father. What it might do to Katy's *mother* was another matter.

She stumbled slightly, and Mack's arm shot out to steady her. Not just to steady her, but to sweep around her waist and practically carry her into her bedroom.

"You're in no condition to even undress yourself,"

he growled. "I'm going to help you, Suzie, so don't argue. I've seen you undressed before, remember, and there's no danger of you falling into my arms in the condition you're in, or of me wanting you to—I'm dead on my feet myself—so let's just get on with it, eh?"

She didn't argue—she was far too worn-out, physically and emotionally. But even in the state she was in, she still felt her skin tingling at the touch of his hands, still felt her breath catch as he pulled her sweater over her head, his warm breath fanning her cheek as he bent over her. And a tiny flame quivered deep inside her as the rest of her clothes followed.

Mack, on the other hand, was treating her disrobing like a clinical exercise. His face was stonily impassive, his eyes narrowed with solemn purpose. He didn't speak or even pause to glance down at her before snatching up a nightgown from under her pillow and slipping it over her head.

But once the task was accomplished, he clamped his hands around her arms and gave her a swift kiss on the lips—too swift for her to even react to.

"Good night, Suzie." He seemed less tense now, more relaxed, as if covering her nakedness had released some of the tension coiled up inside him. "Sleep well. Don't think about anything."

About *them,* did he mean? About what this new development was going to mean to *them?* She stared after him as he turned on his heel and strode out without another word or a backward glance.

Her eyelids drooped. She knew she was far too sleepy right now to grapple with such difficult questions. Best to just fall asleep and dream of Katy. Her tiny, helpless, courageous, beloved Katy.

* * *

As soon as she woke—after six hours dead to the world—she had a quick shower, dressed, and called a cab to take her to the hospital. While she was waiting for it to arrive, she popped down to the boutique to let Priscilla know what was happening—and found out that Prissy had already heard from Mack.

"I'm glad he was here for you, Suzie," Priscilla said blandly, and Suzie gave her a quick, hard look. Prissy knew! Whether she'd guessed or Mack had told her, she knew.

"Yes, me, too," she admitted, but she wasn't going to admit to anything else. Not *yet.* Mack might not be around for long. He might not *want* to stay around. Or she might not want him to.

Her lips curved in a pensive smile. What she wanted and what would be best for Katy were, sadly, two entirely different things.

"You're not to worry about work until Katy's better," Priscilla said firmly. "There's only Amy Braithwaite's wedding dress that's urgent and Sophie can finish it off."

"I'll be home each night," Suzie assured her, "to catch up on—"

"You're not to worry about anything at the moment," Priscilla insisted. "We can manage without you for a few days. Or for as long as you need. Just look after that beautiful baby of yours."

Suzie hugged her. "Thanks, Prissy, you're an angel." She was about to add that it might be possible for her to pop back to the boutique during the day if she and Mack took turns to sit with Katy, but she thought better of it. Mack might have changed his mind by the time she saw him again. *If* she saw him again.

She thought of the way her father had so often promised to do things with her, to come to her concerts and sports days, to take her to a playground or a movie, and instead had gone to the races or the casino, or had sought escape from his frustrations by taking a furious ride on his motorbike, forgetting the promises he'd made to his daughter.

"Ah, here's my taxi," she said, and darted off.

She took deep breaths all the way to the hospital. What if Katy had gone downhill or suffered a serious relapse while she'd been away from her? What if the doctors had been wrong about her recovery? How could she have left her, even for a minute?

She was in a state of nervous panic by the time she reached the isolation ward where Katy should have been. When she found her baby's cot gone, *Katy* gone, she panicked. She rushed to the nurses' station, demanding frantically, "Where's my baby? Where's Katy?"

They calmed her down, telling her that Katy had been moved into intensive care, where she would remain until she was ready to go home. She was fine, they assured her.

Suzie pressed her hands to her chest in relief as she sought out a nurse in intensive care to take her to her baby daughter.

Katy still looked weak and pale—so pale that her ghostly pallor tore at Suzie's heartstrings—and she was still attached to tubes, feeding her the vital antibiotics which would continue until she was well enough to leave the hospital. But her dark eyes fluttered open as Suzie bent over her, almost as if she'd sensed that her mother was there. Suzie felt tears pricking her eyes and emotion welling in her chest as her daughter's pale lips flickered in a smile of recognition.

She would love Mack to have seen that smile, but there was no sign of him. She wondered again if, after a night to reflect on the responsibilities he'd have to face if he stayed around, he'd decided to bow out of their lives. Or—more charitably and hopefully—maybe he was just giving her some time alone with her daughter.

By midmorning she was allowed to hold Katy, tubes and all, while an aide was changing the sheets. The baby seemed to respond to the warm curtain of love enveloping her, her listless dark eyes becoming noticeably brighter, her cheeks even showing traces of color, her tiny hand reaching out to close around her mother's finger.

"She's looking better already," a deep voice commented, and Suzie's head jerked up as she recognized the voice. Not one of the doctors, but—

"Mack!" His name cracked in her throat. Nothing else would come out. He'd come, just as he'd said he would!

He was wearing his black leather jacket again. As always it brought back tantalizing memories—and a flicker of disquiet. *Don't get too carried away at the sight of him. Remember how like your father he is, and what that could mean to Katy's future security and quality of life. And to your own peace of mind.*

She didn't realize her eyes were fastened to his mouth until his lips moved.

"I called the boutique before I came here and Priscilla told me you'd already left to come to the hospital,'' Mack said. ''I thought you would have slept in for hours longer—you had a lot of sleep to catch up on.''

So that was why he hadn't come in earlier. He hadn't expected her to be here yet. Her heart lifted.

''So did you,'' she reminded him. Yet he'd taken the time to call Priscilla first thing this morning, and again just a while ago. ''And I had a solid six hours of sleep,'' she told him. ''It was quite enough. I was anxious to get back here to Katy.''

Mack's dark gaze veered to the baby in her arms. ''She's awake.'' He leaned toward her, but didn't thrust his face too close, not wanting to risk upsetting or unnerving his daughter. ''Brown eyes,'' he commented, and flicked a look at Suzie—a look that said more than any words could.

She gulped down a surge of emotion. ''Nobody could doubt that she's your daughter, Mack.'' She paused, grimacing. ''Though my mother has buried her head in the sand on that particular subject.'' If Ruth knew that Mack was here with her she'd be having a fit.

''So you haven't told your mother that I'm living in Melbourne now?''

Suzie gave a brief, rueful laugh. ''If she knew, she'd probably be over here like a shot to protect me from you.'' Which was why she'd decided against letting her mother know about Katy just yet. She didn't want Ruth rushing over here and causing a scene at the hospital, chasing Mack away before they'd had a chance to sort things out regarding their daughter. The situation was delicate enough as it was.

Mack lifted a dark eyebrow. ''Just what precisely does your mother have against me, Suzie? Is it simply that I wear black leather, ride around on a motorbike, or at least used to, and enjoy an occasional beer?" His tone was sardonic. "She'd like to see me in a smart suit and tie like Tristan Guthrie, working regular hours in a respectable office, is that it?"

Suzie bit down on her lip. She had no heart for a confrontation here, in front of their sick daughter. "Mack, you're here to get to know Katy, not to talk about my mother and what she might think of you." She rocked the baby gently in her arms. "Do you want to hold your daughter?"

But Mack had no chance just then as a nurse swept in to put Katy back to bed, check her vital signs and settle her down for a sleep.

"Why don't you pop down to the cafeteria and grab something to eat?" she suggested, addressing both of them. "Go down before the midday lunch rush."

Suzie hesitated. The way Mack's jaw was set, he looked as if he had more questions to ask and would be demanding answers. Answers she might not be able to give without telling him about—

She heaved in a frayed breath. Her father was dead and gone now. She could no longer hurt his feelings or embarrass her mother by revealing all the sordid details of her father's addictions now. Besides, she'd already accused Mack of gambling, and his reaction, she recalled, had been more of shocked surprise than guilt. She should give him a chance to explain...even knowing how devious gamblers could be.

"Sorry, I need to pop out for a while," Mack said, solving her dilemma. "I have to meet someone."

She should have felt relief, but instead she felt her spirits dip. Despite the questions he must be dying to ask, he was making excuses to get away from her already! Or was he afraid they might end up having a stand-up fight in public over his role in Katy's life? Or with her throwing him out of her life again? And out of Katy's?

Was he really meeting someone, or did he simply want to escape the cloying atmosphere of the hospital for a while? Or maybe his fingers were itching to get back to his computer for an hour or so.

"That's okay. You rush off," she said lightly. Having lunch by herself would suit her just fine, giving her some time to think and get herself together. "I'll be here if Katy needs..." She nearly said *us,* but changed it quickly to "me." She left him without adding, "See you later." If he wanted to come back, he would.

He did. He not only came back, he stayed for the remainder of the afternoon with her. He even held his baby daughter for the first time. Watching him, watching them together, Suzie felt her heartstrings pull tight. He looked so right, so comfortable with her, and Katy didn't even whimper as this dark-eyed, rugged-faced stranger gathered her in his strong arms, ever so carefully, ever so gently, cradling her as if she were a priceless, fragile jewel.

Suzie felt a thickening in her throat. She'd never seen such a tender, glistening warmth in Mack's eyes, or such a softening of his dark, rough-hewn features. The tiny, frail bundle in his arms seemed to have brought this strong, indomitable man to his knees.

"I named her after your mother, Mack," she admitted softly, wanting him to know that she hadn't forgotten him entirely—that she'd wanted her daughter to own at least a part of him. "I named her Katherine Ruth—after both our mothers. After Katy's two grandmothers.''

Mack's dark eyes swept round, impaling hers. He was wondering if he could believe her. ''You didn't even know my mother.''

''No, but the way you always spoke about her—the *loving* way—I knew she meant a lot to you. And you seemed so proud that *you'd* been named after her that I—I wanted Katy to be named after her too.''

Mack smiled, if a trifle ruefully. ''Thanks, Suzie. Good to know I wasn't forgotten altogether.'' But there was a flicker of something in his eyes that showed he was touched by the gesture.

Suzie looked down quickly at her baby daughter, to hide the anguish in her eyes. *Oh, Mack, you were never forgotten, never for a moment!*

It was a relief when one of the nurses interrupted them again. A woman doctor, who introduced herself as Dr. James, was with her. Suzie held her breath as the doctor bent to examine her daughter. *Their* daughter, she corrected. Mack's and hers.

Dr. James declared herself more than satisfied with Katy's progress. The fever had not returned and Katy's tests were all normal, though the antibiotic treatment, of course, would need to continue for a couple of weeks yet.

''You're a lucky couple,'' she said as she left them.

Couple.

Neither disputed the fact that they weren't actually a couple, and perhaps never would be. Suzie gulped as she felt Mack's eyes on her. The dark depths seemed to be telling her that they could have been a couple by now, if she hadn't run out on him all those months ago. There was a glint of raw steel in his eyes.

Was he thinking of those lost months? Or only of the past six, since Katy was born? Six months that he could have spent getting to know his daughter?

Well, it wasn't too late, luckily. Katy was going to be fine, and she *was* only six months old. Mack had plenty of time ahead to get to know his daughter if he wanted to.

She let Mack hold Katy again later in the afternoon, before they both left the hospital for the night. This time his tiny daughter smiled for him, the sweetest smile in all the world. Mack smiled back, and spoke to Katy as any doting father would speak to his baby daughter. And then he looked up and caught Suzie's eyes—and smiled again, this time for *her,* a smile that lit up his dark-browed face and brought a dazzling brilliance to his eyes.

Her heart reeled, and she smiled back—realizing too late that she'd put her heart into her smile...that she'd shown far too much.

"You can't keep me out of your life now, Suzie," Mack said quietly.

She tugged her eyes away from his—which wasn't easy, the compelling force of his gaze making her want to drown in his eyes forever. When he looked at her like that—with that heart-melting warmth in his eyes...

She thought of her father and shivered. Her father could charm her mother with the same ease.

"I'll never keep you out of Katy's," she said in a husky whisper.

Mack didn't speak for a moment, and then, as if satisfied, murmured, "Right. Let's leave it at that until Katy's better. You've enough on your plate right now without having to make life-changing decisions.''

Life-changing decisions. A tremor ran through her. He was telling her he wanted to be in *her* life, not just Katy's. She fingered her throat.

''We'll do what the doctor suggested,'' Mack said gently, ''and take turns coming in here from now on. I can come whenever you want, Suzie. It'll give you a chance to concentrate totally on Katy while you're here with her, and give my daughter a chance to get to know *me* a bit better while I'm here.''

She nodded, looking down at Katy, not at him.

''Maybe we could take in a movie or a show one night,'' Mack suggested. ''Or take a stroll along the river to blow the cobwebs away...''

Her eyes flew to his. ''Mack—''

''I promise not to put any pressure on you, Suzie,'' he was quick to reassure her. ''If you spend all your evenings at home alone, you'll only mope about Katy and work madly until all hours—and Priscilla says you're not to work at night, you're to *rest* and have some fun. Your days will be busy enough tending to Katy and dashing back and forth between your bridal boutique and the hospital. You'll need time in the evenings to unwind.''

As she hesitated, undeniably tempted, he pressed home his advantage. ''I won't make any unwanted advances, if that's what you're afraid of.'' *Unwanted,* she noted with a quiver. ''I won't even come into your flat uninvited. We'll just spend some time together, have a bit of fun, and let our hair down a bit. No hassles,'' he promised again. ''But I think you do owe it to me to tell me about my daughter. About her first six months. About your pregnancy. About your life with Katy."

He cared that much? She looked up at him wonderingly.

Mack let his dark eyes caress her, while keeping his hands, which were itching to caress her in a more tactile way, firmly at his side. "I don't even want you to think about us—you and me—for the next week or so, Suzie," he murmured. "It's our daughter who needs you now. You have to stay fit and fresh and healthy for *her.*"

Our daughter. Yes, thought Suzie, I have to stay strong and fit and healthy for Katy's sake.

"You're right, Mack," she said, her voice husky again. "Katy's all that matters right now."

"I'll drop you home," he offered. "And don't worry," he added with a wry smile as her eyes flared, "I won't come in. I'll pick up some take-away for you on the way. You won't feel like cooking dinner. And don't do any sewing tonight. Get to bed early. You've a lot of sleep still to catch up on."

She didn't argue.

Chapter Ten

They settled into a daily routine, with Suzie coming into the hospital first, around eight, and staying with Katy until Mack arrived later in the morning. Before changing places they would fuss over their baby daughter together—just like a regular mother and father, Suzie thought pensively—keeping their conversation focused on Katy. Then Suzie would dash back to the boutique to see clients, work on her bridal designs, and catch up on her sewing.

By midafternoon she would be back at the hospital, and after quizzing Mack on how Katy had been in her absence, he would drift off, while she stayed with their baby daughter until she was settled down for the night, usually around seven.

Priscilla's husband had insisted on her using one of their cars—Harry owned a secondhand car business—so that she wouldn't have to travel by public transport or pay for taxis. "You never know," Harry said when he delivered the car to her, "you might decide to buy it in the end, so you can look on the next couple of weeks as a test run.''

She was very grateful to him, but she doubted if she'd be able to afford to buy his car—even second-hand.

Mack let her get used to the new routine for a couple of days before suggesting a night out. He'd come prepared, producing two theater tickets and holding them up with a flourish.

''Like to go to a comedy show, Suzie? They say it's hilarious. I want to see you laugh again.'' His dark eyes swept her pale face. ''A good laugh will do you the world of good.''

Her heart picked up a beat. It was too tempting to resist.

''I'd love to go too,'' she heard herself agreeing. ''What time does it start?''

''Eight. I'll come in and relieve you here at five, so you can go home and freshen up. I'll pick you up at your flat at seven-thirty. We can have a light dinner after the show.''

Dinner after the show? She wasn't so sure about that. Wine usually came with dinner, and wine and a starry moonlit night could seduce a woman and muddle her thinking.

''I think I'll be more than ready to fall into bed after the show,'' she warned him, then wished she hadn't mentioned the word *bed,* as a smoldering spark kindled deep in his dark eyes. She flicked her gaze away, settling it on Katy. ''I'll have a snack at home before you pick me up.''

''As you wish.'' He wasn't going to push his luck. ''Well, you'll be wanting to rush off to the boutique....'' He pulled up a chair, close to Katy's cot.

She paused, still amazed at his willingness to give up so much of his time to sit with a sick baby. Would Tristan have been so dedicated? He'd been a real wimp when it came to sickness and needles and the threat of infection. He would have made excuses about being needed at Guthrie Leather Goods—even though he owned the business and could have delegated whenever he wished.

But at least Tristan *had* a job. A *proper* job. She grimaced. She wasn't so sure about *Mack's* current line of work. Was it still going well? Was he still serious about it? He never talked about it, never seemed anxious about the hours he spent away from his computer. Maybe his work only *required* a few snatched hours a day.

"Something wrong, Suzie?"

She jumped. Mack always was uncannily perceptive, she remembered. Far more than Tristan had ever been. "I just hate leaving Katy," she hedged, and bent to kiss her baby daughter—for the third or fourth time—before backing away.

"You're leaving her in good hands, Suzie. I promise," Mack assured her as she turned to leave.

There was a faint dryness in his tone that caused her to falter, and blurt out, "Oh, Mack, I wasn't inferring that you..." She trailed off with a helpless waggle of her hand. She couldn't blame him for thinking she still didn't trust him. She didn't! In certain areas, at least.

But not in this. Not when it came to Katy.

She tossed him a special smile before vanishing through the doorway, letting him know that when it came to Katy she trusted him implicitly.

* * *

Suzie felt Mack's eyes on her several times during the lighthearted show. It was full of lively good humor, catchy songs, and witty one-liners, making her laugh so much she had tears rolling down her cheeks. The final scene was so delightfully funny she had to hold her middle, she was laughing so hard.

She was still chuckling as they filed out. "Oh, that was great, just great," she enthused, her eyes sparkling. "Did you enjoy it, Mack?"

"Sure. But I enjoyed *your* enjoyment more."

He caught her eye for a second, and her heart jumped into her mouth. Remarks like that—*looks* like that—weren't meant to be part of their deal.

"It was just so good to hear you laughing again, and to see the old sparkle back in your eyes," Mack hastened to reassure her. "And to see you enjoying yourself, and letting go for once. Feeling a bit better now?"

She nodded. "I've never laughed so much in my life."

"And it's done wonders for you. Have you noticed all the admiring looks you're getting? That glow on your face is attracting every man's eyes to you. And envious looks from the women."

"Oh, Mack, you do talk rot. They're more likely thinking what a spectacle I made of myself, but I just couldn't stop laughing." Maybe Mack had glanced at her so often during the show because her giggles and loud guffaws were *embarrassing* him. Her laughter had been close to hysterical at times. The release of tension, she guessed. The *need* for release.

Yes, it *had* done her good.

She felt so good that she agreed to go to the theater café with Mack for a light meal before going home, though she was careful to decline a glass of wine. Other theatergoers were packed into the small café like sardines—there was little privacy, which suited her just fine. It made it easy to avoid an intimate conversation. They talked about the show—the performers, the music, the joyous, uplifting fun of it all—until they'd finished their snack and it was time to go home.

On the way, Suzie fell silent, feeling vulnerable again. Would Mack stick to his promise not to come in? Not to put pressure on her? Or would he try to take advantage of her weakened, euphoric state? Would she have the strength to resist him if he did?

She began to tremble. If her mother knew that Mack had reappeared in her life, she'd be regaling her with all the old warnings about getting mixed up with a man who was so like Suzie's irresponsible father, and predicting dire consequences if she did.

And she'd be right, Suzie thought, her spirits slumping. She probably *was* crazy getting mixed up with Mack again.

Not that she had much choice. Having Katy—*Mack's* child—had changed everything. She had to give Mack a chance. She could handle it, she decided, rallying. She was older and wiser these days, and she was fully aware of the dangers of getting involved with him again. She wouldn't be rushing into anything.

As Mack pulled up outside her apartment building, she immediately reached for the door. ''Thanks, Ma—'' she began, and caught her breath as his hand touched her arm. Not gripping it, just touching it.

''Relax, Suzie, I just want to suggest something before you dash off.''

She gulped. "Yes?" It was a hoarse squeak.

His mouth edged into a grin. "You know how Katy always has her longest sleep for the day between eleven and two?"

She nodded. Mack was normally with his daughter at that time. "You'd rather be with her when she's awake for most of the time?" she asked. How selfish she'd been, not to think of that. "Mack, if you want to change shifts..."

He shook his head, his smile gentling. "She's awake for a good part of the afternoon, before you come back in, so I have plenty of waking time with her. No, that's not my point." His dark eyes glimmered in the dimness. "If she's going to be asleep between eleven and two, why don't we grab the chance one day—tomorrow if you like—to slip out for a picnic lunch and a chat about Katy? There's that big park directly behind the hospital."

"Well, I guess." She knew how badly Mack wanted to hear all about his baby daughter. "I'll make some sandwiches."

"There's no need. I'll bring the food." Mack knew a homemade cake shop that made gourmet sandwiches and delicious cakes. "You spend the morning with Katy, and I'll come in at eleven with the goodies. Once she's settled down for her sleep, we'll slip out for an hour or so. Now off you go," he said, drawing back his hand. "I'll wait here until you're safely inside."

She opened the car door, relieved—*or was she?*—that he was sticking to his promise not to come in. Not to make any *unwanted* advances! "Thanks for a lovely night, Mack," she said, and because she'd wronged him, she leaned impulsively toward him, stretched her neck, and gave him a quick kiss on the edge of his mouth.

She didn't give him a chance to react. That could be dangerous. It could risk unraveling the fragile shell she'd wound round her heart. But her body was quivering as she retreated to her apartment, and every pulsing pore was regretting that he hadn't seized her in his arms and brought their lips properly together. A second longer in that car and it might have been too late. She could have thrown all her cautious rules and prudish conditions to the four winds!

Mack sat for a few minutes in his car after she'd gone. He saw her upstairs lights go on and gritted his teeth, trying to curb the stirring in the pit of his stomach. It had taken all the willpower he possessed not to grab her when she reached over to kiss him. If he'd given way to the impulse, he would have kissed her until she was senseless with longing. *For him.*

It would have been so easy. They'd always ignited each other, burned for each other physically. But he didn't want to win her back that way. He wanted her to remember how they'd been together in other ways. How they'd been able to enjoy simple pleasures—each other's company—learning new things about each other—their tastes, their opinions, the things that amused them, upset them or angered them.

He had to be patient. Besides, he'd given her his word. No hassles, no pressure. Not while Katy was sick. To rush her, to go about things the wrong way, could scare her off again. And he couldn't lose her again. Ice clutched his heart at the thought. So far, all was going well. She was allowing him to see Katy and to be alone with his daughter. She'd agreed to go to the theater with him. She'd agreed to have lunch with him in the park tomorrow.

Simple pleasures. That was the way to go. Suzie had had a taste of Tristan's way, the rich man's way, and she'd rejected it. He must keep in mind that she'd rejected *him,* too, once, when he'd tried to impress her with a fistful of easily earned dollars. He wasn't going to make *that* mistake again.

He'd do anything it took.

But damn it, he was only human. She'd better not keep him at arm's length for too long, or he wouldn't be answerable for the consequences!

Suzie was still smiling as she fell into bed. She'd forgotten how much fun she could have with Mack. It wasn't just the show, terrific as it had been. It was being there with Mack, enjoying it with *him.*

They'd always had a good time together, though they'd never been to a top-class show before. Neither of them could have afforded the tickets.

She frowned faintly as she snuggled between the sheets. Tonight they'd had the best seats in the house—the front row of the dress circle, right in the middle. The tickets must have cost Mack a packet.

How had Mack, a newcomer to Melbourne, managed to acquire the best seats in the house? Who did Mack know with the kind of influence that would ensure such preferential treatment?

Oh, Mack, you don't know any Mr. Bigs of the gambling world, do you? Wealthy, powerful men who hand out favors to their regular clients? She buried her face in her pillow.

She had to learn to trust Mack! He could have come by those seats by sheer luck. A last-minute cancellation, perhaps. Mack had always been good at jumping at opportunities and spotting a good bargain. He'd needed to be, had *learned* to be, back in the days when he'd had no job at all.

But the tickets must still have cost him the earth. Could a simple Web editor have earned Mack that kind of money? *It's doing well,* was all he'd said about it. No mention of "a brilliant success," just "doing well."

Maybe he'd spent his last cent on those tickets, to prove to her that he *was* doing well. Tomorrow he'd suggested a simple lunch in the park. That shouldn't cost much. Was that why he'd suggested it?

If Mack only knew that he didn't need to impress her, or spend money on her. He only needed to reassure her that he was always going to be around for her.

Mack joined her at the hospital just before eleven, breezing into intensive care in jeans and an open-necked shirt—not a black one for once, but a mottled gray—his dark hair more ruffled than usual, either tossed about by the breeze or by his own fingers, perhaps, raking through it. He was carrying a bulging plastic bag.

"Our lunch," he said, his dark eyes scanning her face. "Last night did you good, Suzie. You look far more relaxed, and you still have that sparkle." His gaze slid downward. "Nice top," he commented, though it was only a plain blue cotton camisole, suitable for a picnic lunch on a warm September day. It had cost next to nothing.

She was relieved when his gaze flicked up again. But now his eyes were on her tumbled curls, looking as if he'd like to tumble them even further. She felt herself flushing, her heart picking up a beat. Mack had always been good for her morale. She'd never had to pretend to be someone she wasn't with Mack.

"How's Katy?" he asked, approaching the cot.

"She's coming along beautifully." She could feel her face taking on a new glow. For Katy. "She's been bouncing around all morning. They're very pleased with her. I've just put her down. She'd tired herself out."

"Fast asleep already." Mack's dark eyes softened as he gazed down at his baby daughter. "I won't disturb her." He straightened. "So you reckon she might sleep for a couple of hours?" His eyes took on a different gleam as they swung to her.

She felt a flutter of excitement, a wicked thrill, as if they were about to play truant from school. "I wouldn't be surprised if she sleeps for a solid two and a half hours at least."

"Then let's go. It's a perfect day for a picnic."

They found a garden seat under some shady gum trees. Mack delved into his plastic bag, pulling out packs of sandwiches and fancy cupcakes.

"I threw in a couple of bottles of soft drink, as well. I thought we'd better not breathe alcohol over Katy. The sisters mightn't approve."

Suzie gave a tentative smile. He was going all out to show her that he was a responsible father...a responsible husband. She wanted to believe it—*how* she wanted to!—but she kept remembering how her charming father had tried to hide his vices, too, in the beginning...until he was caught in their trap and sank from despair to rock bottom, dragging his wife and daughter into his private hell with him.

The reminder rather blighted what might have been a thoroughly pleasant couple of hours.

The following night, after a quick pasta meal at an Italian place in town, Mack took her to a movie. It was a light romantic comedy, and she loved it. Mack, she knew, preferred action movies, but if he was bored, he didn't show it. As with the stage show the other night, he seemed to enjoy *her* enjoyment.

And her company?

A sigh quivered from her. His consideration for her, his lethal closeness, and his endless interest in everything Katy had done in her young life from the moment she was born—and even before she was born—were becoming dangerously, irresistibly seductive.

She longed to be back in Mack's arms. Longed to give herself fully to him, as she had that one time before—that momentous time. But on that occasion she'd been emotionally fragile and hadn't been thinking straight and she'd tumbled out of control. She didn't want to be out of control the next time—for Katy's sake. She wanted to be very sure of what she was doing, what she was getting herself into.

"How about we go to Southbank tomorrow night, after dinner?" she suggested a couple of nights later as Mack dropped her home after an evening at a suburban pub, famous for its sensational jazz band. "It would be nice to take a stroll along the river at night," she said carelessly, "and watch those dramatic flames that shoot up along the banks of the river, by the casino. I've never been there at night."

"Sure, why not?" Mack's eyes didn't even flicker at her mention of the casino—though it was dim in his car and she might have missed it. "Why don't we have dinner at Southbank first? There are lots of good restaurants."

She shook her head. "I promised to have dinner at the hospital with some of the nurses. Do you realize Katy will be coming home in a couple of days?" Happiness and relief welled in her throat, her eyes shining at the thought of having her baby daughter safely home again. At last.

Mack felt for her hand and gave it a squeeze, his warmth enveloping her. "Yeah, it's great, isn't it? And coming home healthy and strong. We're very lucky parents. A very lucky family," he added deliberately, his dark eyes catching and holding hers.

Suzie swallowed. *We...parents...family...* Mack was thinking of them as a *family* now? She felt too choked up to answer. If only! If only dreams and fairy tales and one's deepest wishes could come true. Her life, so far, had taught her otherwise.

"And you're looking far healthier and stronger yourself, Suzie. Having some time off and a few laughs has done you the world of good."

She nodded, knowing they had. And she had Mack to thank for it.

When Mack's face moved closer she didn't turn her head away or make a panicky lunge for the door. She let him kiss her, long and lingeringly, hoping it might ease some of the tension that had been mounting between them with each passing day.

She didn't let it go beyond a kiss, though it took all her willpower to pull out of his arms and send him on his way. It was lucky they were in his car, and not in her flat. She might not have been so strong-minded within the cozy walls of her home.

But his kiss, instead of easing the tension, only made her want him more.

She could feel the silken net tightening, weaving deep into her heart and soul, and she wasn't sure that it was such a bad thing anymore. She loved Mack, she always had, and now she had a powerful reason to keep him in her life. His baby daughter recognized him now and looked forward to his visits. How could she limit Mack to occasional access visits? *Did she want to?*

She trembled as she locked herself inside her lonely flat. Maybe tomorrow night would answer the question nagging her the most.

Hell, did she know what she was doing to him? Mack was so aroused he could barely drive home. Being with her tonight had been sheer torture. Sheer delight and sheer torture. But he mustn't blow things by doing anything stupid. He'd promised to give her time, promised not to pressure her, at least while Katy was still in hospital.

He didn't have long to wait now…just a couple of days…

But there was a limit to what a man could take.

They stood on the footbridge spanning the Yarra River at Southbank, looking upstream to the grand old Princes Bridge.

"I never realized Melbourne could be so beautiful," Suzie breathed, drinking in the amber-lit Victorian buildings on either side of the river and their dazzling reflections in the glassy-still water. "Paris, along the Seine, couldn't be more beautiful than this."

Mack slipped an arm around her shoulders and she didn't shake it off, finding it protective and deliciously sexy at the same time. It made her want to sink into him, but she managed to resist, gripping the rail instead.

"We'll have to go there one day and find out...you and me and Katy." He turned to face her, his eyes challenging her. Challenging her to deny him a place in Katy's life. In *her* life.

As she stopped breathing, he held up his hands. "Sorry. Does that come under the heading Heavy Stuff? Or Pressure?"

She swallowed a lump in her throat. Traveling to the other side of the world with Mack and Katy sounded wonderful. Was it an impossible dream? It would be expensive, and would mean time off work. Now that she had a daughter, Katy's long-term security had to be her primary concern.

She flicked a shoulder. "Yes, well, it'll have to stay a dream for now, won't it?" Another of Mack's pipe dreams.

"Let's take a look at the casino," she suggested, her gaze veering downriver to the glitzy, neon-lit, Las Vegas-style gambling complex. They'd already had coffee at a riverside café and wandered through the vast Southbank shopping complex, admiring a lot of overpriced designer gear that Suzie felt she could have reproduced at half the price.

"Well, if you like." Mack looked surprised. "I didn't think you'd be interested."

"I've never been inside a casino." She probed his dark eyes, but all she saw was that flicker of surprise. If there was a gleam of excitement or anticipation there, too, he was hiding it well.

But then, her father had hidden his vice well, too, in the early days of his addiction.

They entered the casino to a blaze of color and jangling sound and hazy, swirling smoke. Suzie felt herself recoiling. This was the glitzy, tacky world her father had inhabited. The world of poker machines and gambling tables and frantic, addicted gamblers. She wanted to turn and run, but instead she grabbed Mack's arm and said with feigned eagerness, "Let's have a go on the pokies—just for fun." There were rows and rows of them, luring them with their bright lights and harsh sounds.

He gave her a whimsical smile. "Well, if you really want to..."

"I do! Don't you?" she asked lightly. She wanted to know...to be sure....

He shrugged. "Whatever makes you happy."

He wasn't reacting the way she'd expected. Maybe poker machines were child's play to him. On an impulse, she changed tack. "Come to think of it, the gambling tables would be more exciting. What should we play? What did you play when you were in Las Vegas?"

He glanced at her. "I didn't play the tables," he reminded her mildly.

Suzie could read nothing from his expression. "Well, what did you play when you won all that money at the Sydney casino that time?"

Mack's eyes narrowed. Why was she reminding him of that long-ago night, *the night she'd walked out on him?* Did his big win, his far-too-easy win, still rankle with her? Well, there was no way he was going to fall into the same trap. If she wanted to gamble, fine. He intended to stay safely out of it.

"From memory, it was roulette," he said. "You want to have a flutter, do you?"

"Why not? You can show me what to do. Let's get some chips."

She was horrified when she found out that the lowest single bet you could have was five dollars. "I'm prepared to risk twenty dollars," she said, sadly aware that she couldn't really spare that. "That'll give me four chances."

Mack gave a crooked grin. "You won't get far with that. Here's another twenty," he offered, and as she opened her mouth to protest, "and there's no need to pay me back unless you win a fortune." His tone was sardonic, as if he couldn't see that happening. "If you play carefully, going for fifty-fifty chances, you'll have a better chance than if you put your money on a single number and hope it comes up. But you won't win as much."

"Is that how you had your big win? By putting your chips on a single number?"

He shrugged. "Don't follow my example or you could lose the lot," he advised. "I was just lucky. Put five dollars on the red or the black and see what happens."

Deciding to play it safe, she chose the black. It came up red. "There's five dollars gone," she said pouting, and realized just how quickly one could lose money at the tables. She tried black again, and this time it came up, though the return was disappointingly small.

"Aren't you going to join me?" she asked Mack. Surely, if he was a secret gambler, he'd be itching to have a few bets?

"I have joined you. I'm right beside you."

"Oh." She decided to be more adventurous, thinking it might prove too tempting for Mack and entice him to play himself. "I'll try putting it on a line of numbers this time." She did, and had another win. And another after that. A flukish run of wins followed.

Then she panicked.

"Let's get out of here," she gasped, and stumbled away from the crowded table.

"Aren't you going to pick up your winnings?" Mack asked. "Here, give me your chips. I'll do it."

He came back with a handful of notes. Suzie picked out a twenty-dollar note and handed it to him. "Thanks for the loan," she said stiffly, and after pocketing twenty dollars for herself, she stuffed her remaining winnings into a box to go to some charity she barely took in.

"That's generous of you," Mack remarked.

She jerked a shoulder. "Easy come, easy go. Can we go now?" she pleaded, regretting her impulse to come here.

"Sure. Suits me. The crowd and the smoke too much for you?"

She nodded, though her panic had nothing to do with the crowd or the smoke. What had really terrified her was the fear that if she had any more wins she might become addicted like her father. For a few seconds she'd felt the excitement a gambler must feel when he has a run of wins, and she'd felt herself choking with fear and disgust.

So much for putting temptation in *Mack's* way. Mack hadn't even had a bet, hadn't shown the faintest desire to. But that was *good,* she thought in the next breath. If he'd been truly addicted to gambling, surely he would have wanted a few bets himself—especially as *she* was playing and openly inviting him to join her?

As they made their way through the crowd, Suzie saw a tall redheaded man waving to them over the heads in front. She'd never seen the man in her life before, so concluded he was waving to Mack.

"I think a friend of yours is beckoning to you," she said, glancing up at Mack.

He gave a grimace, and suddenly steered her away, hurrying her to a different exit.

"Mack, what's going on?" she gasped. "Who was that man?"

"Just someone I'd rather not see."

Her breath snagged in her throat. *A man at the casino he didn't want to see.* She clenched her hands into tight fists. Not a *gambling* buddy, she begged silently—a buddy who might open his mouth and spill the beans on Mack's secret gambling habits! Or even worse, a *debt collector.* Someone Mack owed money to for gambling debts!

Why else would Mack be so secretive, so anxious to avoid the man?

Her night thoroughly ruined now, she demanded to be taken home. She barely talked on the way. As Mack pulled up outside her apartment, he caught her arm, preventing her immediate escape.

"You're not still worried about that guy I avoided at the casino, are you?"

She turned slowly, her heart constricting as she wondered what was coming. A string of lies? Or finally, the truth?

"Is there some reason you can't tell me who he is?" she asked, unable to hide the tremor in her voice.

He hesitated, and her heart constricted a bit more. "He's a windbag," he said with a shrug. "A colossal bore. We would never have been able to get away from him."

She wondered if she could believe him. Mack wasn't the type to suffer fools gladly. If he'd wanted to get away from someone he found a bore, he would simply have made some excuse and walked away.

"Oh, Mack," she said helplessly, wondering if she would ever know the real Mack Chaney, or ever be able to trust him. For Katy's sake, she dearly wanted to be able to. *For her own sake, too.* "Just when I think I'm beginning to know you." She shook her head. "I—I don't think I'll ever know you properly!" She heaved a sigh. With her father's history, wouldn't that be too big a risk to take?

"Suzie, you have to learn to trust me," Mack said, his voice a deep rumble in the close confines of his car. "You have to let go of your past and learn to trust your own instincts." He brushed a hand over her hair, then down her cheek, with a finger-light touch of infinite gentleness. "Do you honestly think I'd ever do anything to harm you? Or our daughter?"

Our daughter. She looked up into his eyes—a dark, ebony glitter in the dimness. No, she couldn't imagine Mack ever harming a hair of Katy's head. Or her own, for that matter. Not deliberately. But her father hadn't intended to hurt her either. Or her mother.

"Suzie, now that Katy's well again and ready to come home, it's time we had a talk. About *us,*" Mack said, in a tone that a woman would argue with at her peril.

She panicked again, even though she knew it couldn't be avoided any longer. "Not now," she breathed. "It's too late. I'm too tired." *And too emotionally frazzled.* And she would feel too exposed and vulnerable here in Mack's car or up in her flat. If he took her into his arms she might not *want* to talk. And they had to!

"Tomorrow night," she promised shakily, knowing she couldn't fob him off any longer. Katy would be coming home the following day.

But would she have the strength to keep her head and have a rational, dispassionate discussion, and not fall into Mack's arms as she longed to do?

She would have to!

"How about meeting at a restaurant?" Mack suggested, sensing her panic. "A quiet place where we can talk over dinner."

She nodded, relieved. Dinner, with other people around, should be safe enough. He wasn't inviting himself to her flat. Or her to *his.* She wouldn't even be able to *think* if she was in an intimate flat alone with him. Especially if he seized her in his arms and—

She blotted out the erotic, mind-numbing images that curled through her. No. To be alone with him would be fatal. She had to be in a place where she could keep her wits about her. She had to be able to think—and she would need to think very rationally and very carefully or Mack Chaney would be able to talk her into anything.

Just as his touch, his kisses, or a sexy, provocative look, could make her want to *do* anything!

Chapter Eleven

Suzie left the hospital a few minutes earlier than usual, wanting to shower and change before Mack picked her up at seven-thirty. She needed to gather her strength for the evening ahead.

She was surprised to find Priscilla still at the boutique.

"Ah, Suzie, I was just packing up, ready to go home. Tell me the latest on Katy. Is she still coming home tomorrow?"

"Yes!" Suzie's heart soared. "And I can hardly wait." She launched into details, her relief evident in every excited breath she took.

"It's great that she's doing so well," Priscilla said warmly. "And...your friend Mack?" she asked tentatively. Suzie had barely mentioned him as she'd rushed between the hospital and the boutique each day, and Prissy had usually left the boutique by the time she came home from the hospital of an evening.

She took a deep breath. "Prissy...I don't really

want to talk about Mack…not yet. There's too much to resolve, and I don't know what's going to happen yet."

"Well, I hope things turn out the way you want, Suzie. Talking about Mack Chaney, do you happen to know if he has a brother called Stephen? Or a cousin?"

Suzie pursed her lips. "He has a sister living in New Zealand, but no brothers. I don't know about a cousin."

"Well, maybe Stephen Chaney's a cousin. Chaney's not a terribly common name, is it, so they could well be related. I noticed the posh car Mack was driving when he picked you up one night." Her eyes twinkled. "Maybe his cousin Stephen has given him a handout."

A *handout?* Suzie's heart sank. A handout would mean that Mack hadn't earned the money himself to buy his new car.

But it would also mean that he hadn't won the money in a windfall at the casino…*gambling.*

"What are you talking about, Prissy?" she demanded. "Why would this Stephen Chaney character be giving handouts to anybody? Has he just won the lottery or something and become an instant millionaire?"

"No, he hasn't won the lottery. He earned his fortune by his own genius, and in an amazingly short time, according to the glowing write-up on him in this morning's paper. In less than two years he's become a millionaire several times over."

Prissy rummaged around for a moment in the clutter and pulled out a folded section of newspaper. "I kept the article to show you. Stephen Chaney's the founder of a new Australian company called Digger Software—which, it seems, has turned into a positive gold mine.''

''A computer company?'' Suzie's brow rose. Computer brains must run in the Chaney family. If Stephen and Mack *were* related.

''That's right. It's only a small company so far, but it's taken off like wildfire. Stephen Chaney has over thirty people working for him already. His company produces, quote—world-class Internet tools—unquote.''

Suzie shrugged. ''Never heard of it. I don't normally read the business section. Or the computer pages.''

''Neither do I, but this article was in the main section. And the headline, Computer Whiz a Multimillionaire at Twenty-Nine leapt out at me.''

Twenty-nine? Computer whiz? Suzie's heart missed a beat. *Mack* was twenty-nine. And *he* was a computer whiz. Or at least he'd been coming up with hot new ideas on his computer for as long as she'd known him. Not that any of them had come to anything until his latest invention...the Web editor he'd been selling over the Internet. But that was just a software package. Digger Software was a *company,* employing a staff of over thirty people.

And besides, Mack had been at the hospital every day for the past two weeks—at least for part of the day—not absorbed with running a successful company, for heaven's sake!

''It all started from a simple idea, apparently,'' Priscilla raved on. ''He created some Internet product called Cobber, which took off like mad and is now being used all over the world. It's Digger Software's main product.''

''Is there a photograph of this Stephen Chaney?'' Suzie asked, her voice slightly husky. If only, she thought. If only...

But it was impossible. Mack's name was not Stephen Chaney. *My parents named me Mack after my mother, Katherine Mack,* he'd told her.

And besides—oh, it was laughable that she was even *thinking* it—Mack would have told her if he'd formed a company with a staff of thirty and become a millionaire virtually overnight. He'd be shouting it from the rooftops, letting his doubters—her, her mother, his friends, whoever would listen—know that he'd finally hit the jackpot he'd talked about for so long.

Still, it was pleasant to dream. If Stephen Chaney could make millions from a simple idea in less than two years, maybe Mack could, too, given time. He wasn't thirty yet. How many men became millionaires—or even moderately successful—before the age of thirty?

''A photo?'' Priscilla shook her head. ''Not of Stephen Chaney, no. There's a photo of his media spokesman instead—some guy who works in his public relations department. Here, take it.'' Priscilla thrust the newspaper at her. ''You can show it to Mack and ask him about it. If you intend to see him again,'' she added guilelessly.

Suzie gave a lopsided grin. ''He's taking me out to dinner tonight,'' she admitted, and sighed, the tension she'd been trying to ease gripping her again. ''We—um—have things to talk over.''

''You only intend to *talk?*'' Prissy's eyes danced.

''Be pretty hard to concentrate on talk, wouldn't it, with that sexy, dark-eyed devil?''

''Prissy, you're fishing again.'' Suzie stood up, the folded newspaper in her hand. ''I'd better go and freshen up. I'm dying for a hot shower.'' A reviving shower to prepare her for the evening ahead.

She paused only long enough to hear Priscilla's latest update on their bridal clients, then she gave Prissy a hug and ran upstairs.

She tossed the folded newspaper down on the sofa and headed straight for the bathroom. She could read it later. Or take the article with her, to ask Mack about it over dinner. Maybe Stephen Chaney's success would inspire *him.* And show him what was possible if he worked hard enough and applied his high-blown ideas to the real world.

She chewed on her lip as she stood under the hot shower. Maybe, on second thought, it would be best *not* to show Mack the article, or even mention it. He might think she was having a shot at him. That she wanted *him* to become a multimillionaire like his Chaney namesake, or to aim for heights that were unattainable.

She didn't! She just wanted Mack to have a solid, satisfying job and a secure future. If Mack never became rich and successful, she wouldn't care. Wealth and power, she'd come to realize, could be just as destructive. Look at Tristan Guthrie, thinking he was so rich and powerful he could flaunt the law and get away with it.

She winced as she contemplated Mack's possible reaction to the article. Embarrassment, or even shame, at his own lack of success? Jealousy of Stephen Chaney's, his namesake's, overnight success? Indignation, anger even, that she was comparing him to more successful men?

No! She couldn't hurt him that way.

Having come to her decision, she switched off the shower, rubbed herself dry, and stood for a moment, wondering what to wear. She settled for black slacks and a pale-blue sweater with a modestly scooped neckline. She put on a little makeup and a pink lipstick, then brushed her hair until it shone, leaving her curls as they fell. She didn't want to overdo it and make it look like a date. Tonight was simply an opportunity to talk.

Talk? She gave a rueful snort. It was also wrought with danger, heart-stopping uncertainties, and a heady, spine-tingling excitement!

Her intercom buzzed on the dot of seven-thirty. She felt a zing of anticipation, a rush of renewed tension.

"Mack?"

His voice came back, the familiar, faintly teasing drawl. "You were expecting someone else?"

"No, Mack," she breathed. She wouldn't *want* anyone else. She didn't need tonight's "talk" to know that. *You have to learn to trust me,* Mack had said. She was trying so hard.

Grabbing her purse, she darted down the stairs, almost tripping over her own feet in her rush to reach him.

She swung the door open and there was Mack in his favorite black leather, his shimmering black eyes and broad-shouldered frame lit up by the outside light.

Their eyes met and the earth tilted. Suzie's vocal cords stuck in her throat. She couldn't seem to breathe. It was as if something between them had shifted to another plane.

Mack was the first to speak, a betraying hoarseness in his voice. "Why don't we stay right here, Suzie, and get a pizza delivered? It's hard to have a deep, meaningful conversation in a restaurant. There'd be less distractions here." A tiny flame smoldered in his eyes.

Her heart fluttered a warning. Being in her flat with just Mack was precisely what she'd been trying to avoid. How would she ever be able to think straight with no bustling restaurant to provide a safety buffer?

She dragged her gaze away from the compelling lure of his, but she could feel herself weakening. There was sense in what he'd said. They *would* be able to talk more easily alone in the flat, if she could only keep Mack's mind on what needed to be said. And if she could only keep her *own* mind on matters of the head—and not the heart!

What she mustn't do was give Mack the slightest chance to take her into his arms, because she knew what would happen if he did. Practical matters would simply cease to matter. Until too late, perhaps.

Still wavering in her mind—her sensible, logical mind—she heard herself answering coolly, "Well, if you like, but the flat's in a mess." Then, realizing this was Mack she was talking to she added, "You should feel right at home."

"I always feel at home with you, Suzie."

She flushed. She'd walked right into that one! "Well, I'm warning you, I've left all my sewing out. And the place is littered with newspapers I haven't had time to read yet."

She felt her cheeks heating as she remembered the

newspaper that Priscilla had given her earlier. Where had she left it? She couldn't remember. If Mack saw it and thought she'd left it out deliberately, to show him up…

She groaned inwardly. She might have done that a year ago, but not now that she'd seen him with his daughter. Now that she knew her feelings for him were as strong as ever—stronger—despite the doubts that still lingered. She loved him so much she would never want to do anything that might hurt or humiliate him.

Besides, Mack *had* changed. He was no longer the aimless, unemployed biker he'd been in the past. His new product—his Web editor—must be doing well for him to be invited to talk about it at a convention in Las Vegas. And he owned a BMW! However he'd attained it—from a rich cousin, from a win at the casino, or by his own efforts—he could obviously afford to keep it and run it.

But she knew that Mack's income, large or small, wasn't the problem. It was what he intended to do with the money he earned that made her wary, and hesitant to accept him back in her life with open arms. Was he still gambling? Still drinking? There'd been no hint of alcohol on his breath on any of his visits to the hospital, but how could you tell if someone was secretly *gambling?*

Her own father had always managed to hide his secret vice from the world, with the help of Suzie's hardworking mother, who'd always covered up for him and had bailed him out of trouble time and time again. But the fights and the frustration and the despair!

Suzie shivered. Could she, loving Mack as she did, ignore her own family history and risk a similar fate to her mother?

Could she?

Chapter Twelve

The moment they walked into her flat, Suzie began rushing about, snatching up newspapers and fabric scraps and half-finished garments, thinking that by keeping her hands busy she could help to settle her wildly jumping nerves.

"Don't tidy up on my account," Mack drawled. "I'm used to mess, remember?"

Oh, yes, she remembered. She remembered everything—the bad as well as the good. That was part of the trouble.

She seized on a diversion. "Do you miss your old family home, Mack?" she asked. Messy and run-down as it had been, it must have held nostalgic memories for him—memories of his father and his mother and of her, too, perhaps. She felt quite nostalgic herself about the old house. It was where she'd first met and fallen in love with Mack, and where she'd conceived Katy....

Mack gave a shrug. He'd only missed Suzie.

Missed her like hell. "It was almost falling down around me. I can't say I miss it too much. I've found it's rather pleasant living here in Melbourne—in a modern flat without a lot of clutter."

Her eyes widened. "You live without any clutter? That I'd like to see!" She winced as the words left her lips. She hadn't meant—

"You can see it any time you like, Suzie. But it's only a rented apartment. I'm hoping to buy a house soon, as a permanent home. But that rather depends on you." His eyes pierced hers for a breath-stopping second.

A permanent home...depends on you... The words spun in her brain. He wanted to settle down? With her? And Katy?

"Mack—" she began, and paused, wondering how to broach the doubts and uncertainties that still niggled her.

"Suzie, stop bustling around like a chicken with its head cut off and come and sit down." Mack had already flopped down on the couch and was patting the cushion next to him. "We have a lot to thrash out and I'd like your total attention."

She looked at his strong brown hand on the cushion and knew that if she sat down with him, if she let him touch her, or even brush his arm against hers, she wouldn't care about thrashing out anything. She would weakly say yes to whatever he suggested.

She dragged up a chair facing him. His smoldering black eyes, devouring her as she sat down, were just as potent as his body, but at least she'd put some space between them.

"Suzie, I know why you can't trust me. Why you're afraid to trust me." Mack came straight to the point. "You've had a rotten time with your father, and you've equated me with him."

She didn't deny it. She *was* afraid to trust Mack, at least with her head and cold logic. In her heart and soul, she'd always trusted him and always would.

"Your mother's wrong about me, you know. I'm not like your father," Mack said flatly. "Okay, I was a bit wild in the past—I loved to ride my Harley, I sometimes drank too much, and I played around. But I've changed since then. I changed when I met you, Suzie. Those days are over. I'll still have a beer with a mate or a wine with dinner, but I don't drink to excess," he stressed. "And I never drink and drive. Even in my wild youth I never rode my bike if I'd been drinking beyond the limit." He quirked an eyebrow. "Have you ever seen me drunk?" he challenged.

She hesitated, remembering the night he'd come home from the casino reeking of whiskey and rolling in money, and how unnaturally exhilarated he'd been—reminding her of her father during one of his rare highs, before he'd plunged into an alcohol-induced depression.

She broached the subject carefully, knowing from bitter experience how touchy and evasive secret drinkers and gamblers could be. "That night you had your big win at the casino, Mack, back in Sydney..." A hint of the old disdain shimmered in her eyes. "You must have been gambling and drinking all night!"

Mack stared at her. "*That's* what's been bothering you? That's why you made that crack earlier about gambling my money away?" He pursed his lips, his eyes narrowing. "Your father was a gambler?" His gaze held hers, demanding the truth.

It was out at last. She shuddered, and gave a brief nod. She still felt disloyal admitting it. Disloyal to her mother, and disloyal to her father's memory.

"My mother always tried to boost Dad's self-respect by covering up his gambling...and his other troubles. He—he wasn't a bad man, Mack," she assured him huskily. "He was just terribly frustrated and depressed because his paintings weren't appreciated. He had his own style that didn't appeal to a lot of people. When he did make a sale, he—he would gamble away the money he'd earned, trying to make more...for *us,* he said. Sometimes he *would* win more, but mostly he'd lose it and sink deeper into debt. In the end he became so addicted he lost all control." A tremor shook through her.

"And you think that after that one big win at the casino, I became addicted like your father?"

She flinched under the scornful disbelief in his eyes. "You *could* have," she whispered. "Are you telling me you've never gambled since?"

"Never." There was no hesitation. "I've never had any desire to."

She eyed him doubtfully. She wanted so much to believe him! "My father used to deny it, too," she said hesitantly, voicing her long-held qualms aloud. "That's part of the addiction. Denying you're addicted."

"I'm not addicted, Suzie. Gambling leaves me cold. You can ask anyone."

"But you can't deny that you went to the casino to gamble that night," she challenged. "If gambling leaves you cold, why did you go there? You can't deny you were over the moon with your massive win—or that you'd had a few too many drinks. I've never known you to be so *loud.*'' Her mouth twisted. ''The happy drunk. Just like my father used to be before he sank into one of his black depressions.''

Mack's chest rose and fell in a sigh. ''Let me tell you about that night, Suzie. I was doing some free-lance computer work at the time to make ends meet after I tossed in my job with that computer firm. The casino invited me in one night to do some work on their computers. They had a serious problem and their own guys hadn't been able to solve it. I fixed the problem, and they were so grateful, they gave me a generous bonus on top of a sizable check for work done well. The bonus was in the form of gambling chips.''

''You could have cashed them in.''

''Yeah, I could. But I already had a very generous check and I had no intention of gambling that away. And I didn't. But I decided to be sociable and have a flutter. If I lost, I'd still have the check. Okay,'' he conceded, ''I was in a relaxed frame of mind. They'd insisted on celebrating my success over a few drinks and I'd had a couple of whiskies. Being more used to beer than spirits, I was happy. But I wasn't drunk. As soon as I scored that big freak win, I left.''

''And came straight round to my place,'' Suzie said unsteadily, ''gloating about your great win at the casino. And reeking of whiskey.''

Mack sighed, a rueful half smile on his lips. ''I was so sure you'd be happy for me, Suzie. Having some money for a change—a lot of money. But you acted as if I'd robbed a bank and told me you never wanted to see me again. I assumed you thought I was trying to *buy* your love by big-noting about my sudden windfall.''

He held up a hand as her lips parted. ''It hit me then that I really had nothing solid or long-term to offer you. I had no steady job, no steady income and no bright prospects for the future.''

''Oh, Mack.'' Suzie leaned forward, longing to reach out to him, but not daring to—not yet. Once she touched him… ''It was the gambling more than your prospects,'' she admitted brokenly, ''though I admit that my mother—''

''Had warned you never to marry for love alone,'' Mack finished for her, his tone dry. ''And I had nothing but love to offer you.''

''Oh, Mack, you had far more,'' she cried, ''but I didn't see it back then. I was afraid you were like my father, and that you'd sink into despair because your ideas weren't taking off and you weren't making a success of your life, and that you'd end up addicted to drink and gambling as an escape. I thought that—that history would repeat itself!''

She didn't realize she'd moved from her upright chair until she found that she was sitting on the couch beside Mack, gripping his arm. ''But you're nothing like my father. I see that now.''

''No, I'm not.'' Steady black eyes caught and held hers. ''I'm not a gambler, Suzie. I didn't gamble away that money I won, or the check I earned. I invested it, and lived off it while I was working on my Web editor. And I'm not a big drinker,'' he repeated.

She chewed on her lip. ''You—you mentioned that you're more used to drinking beer than spirits,'' she ventured, anxious to clear up her last doubt, ''but you had an open bottle of whiskey in your cupboard the day I was there, and you gulped down a whole glass in one swallow."

"There was very little whiskey in that glass, Suzie." He actually looked *amused,* not the least perturbed—certainly not sly or defensive, as her father had so often looked. And thinking back, his glass that night had held even less than her own, and he'd followed it up with coffee, not another drink.

"And I'd had that bottle of whiskey for ages," Mack added easily. "I keep a bottle on hand to offer guests. Or females in distress."

He let that sink in for a moment, then repeated levelly, "I'm nothing like your father, Suzie." He slanted his head at her. "History is not going to repeat itself, because your father and I are two totally different men. I am not going to end up like him, and if you and I do decide to get together, you won't have the kind of life you had with him, I promise you. Do you believe me?"

"Yes," she said without hesitation, feeling ashamed now of her doubts. She did more than just believe him. Instinctively, she *knew* that everything he'd just told her was the truth. Scales had been lifted from her eyes...the scales her mother had put there...the scales her tormented father had put there. It was as if she were seeing Mack for the first time as he really was, no longer viewing him through distorted images of her father or the warning face of her mother.

Mack as he really was.

She smiled, even daring to make a quip. "How can you be like my father," she teased, "when you've sold your Harley? Even at his lowest ebb, when we were stony broke and in serious debt, my father never considered parting with his beloved motorbike. Why *did* you sell yours?'' she asked curiously. ''You could have bought a cheaper car than a BMW, and kept your bike. And had both.''

''You don't like my car?''

''It's a beautiful car. It runs like a dream. But there must be less expensive cars that run just as well. And then you needn't have sold your bike.''

''I didn't want to keep the bike. I thought it would be a constant reminder to you of your father, Suzie, and the way he died.''

As her eyes flicked to his, glistening with the sheen of unshed tears—not for her tragic father so much as for Mack's thoughtful gesture in sacrificing his precious bike for *her* sake—Mack drawled, ''As for the BMW, I was thinking of *you* when I bought it.'' The corner of his mouth curved upward. ''Thinking what car *you* would like. A reliable car. A sensible, comfortable sedan, with room for a family eventually.''

His eyes burned into hers and her heart turned over. A family? He'd been thinking of her? And a *family?* He wouldn't have known about Katy then.

''I was determined to win you back, Suzie. I knew you couldn't have married anyone else, because you were still married to me and hadn't asked for a divorce. But when I saw your baby, and you let me think it was another man's—'' A betraying spark lit the dense black of his eyes.

He hissed in his breath. ''Do you love me, Suzie?'' A muscle twitched in his cheek.

She nodded, her answer in the glistening radiance of her eyes. ''I do, Mack...I'll always love you. Love was never the problem,'' she admitted soberly.

"Ah, no..." For a second the brooding look was back. "*Never marry for love alone,* your mother always drummed into you. And what about now?" His voice was a deep, soft, compelling rumble. "Now that you know that I'm not a drunk or a gambling addict or a useless, layabout biker? Would you be prepared to live as my wife now, Suzie. For keeps? Or are you still on the lookout for a man as rich and handsome and socially impeccable as Tristan Guthrie?"

"I would never want another man like Tristan Guthrie," she said with feeling. Her hand trembled on his arm. *For keeps,* he'd said. Suddenly she longed to touch him in other places, his tough, strong-jawed face, his muscled chest, his flat stomach, his... She snapped off her thoughts before she was tempted to put them into wicked action. She had to reassure Mack first!

"And no, Mack, I'm not on the lookout for a man with oodles of money, glossy film-star looks and a gold-plated background." Her eyes roved lovingly over Mack's rugged features, his spellbinding black eyes, the dark, brooding slash of his eyebrows.

"All I want is a man who loves me as much as I love him," she breathed huskily, "and who will love my daughter—*his* daughter—just as much. Someone whose brilliant computer mind will enable him to make a reasonable living, which will be important for his self-respect and peace of mind, though he'll have my help, too, mind. I'd like to continue designing bridal gowns."

She gazed up at him with warmly shining eyes. "That, Mack, is all I want. Just you and Katy. *If* you mean it." She slanted her head at him, her honeyed curls bobbing. "You truly want to settle down and become a husband, a father and a staid old family man?" *And my lover?* she added silently, a tiny thrill riffling through her.

"You still have doubts about me?" Mack sighed, but his own eyes were smiling, a tender flame glowing in their depths. "Well, I guess I can't blame you. I haven't been *entirely* honest with you. Oh, God, don't look at me like that," he begged, gathering her in his arms. "It's nothing bad. At least, I hope it's not."

She raised her face to his, trying to still her heartbeat as she wondered what could be coming. But something in his eyes reassured her. "I know it won't be bad, Mack," she whispered. "I trust you. Whatever it is."

He touched her cheek with gentle fingers, sending tingling shivers right down to her toes. "You told me once that you wanted a man you could rely on," he reminded her. "I thought you meant that you wanted a man you could rely on *financially.* But that was never what you meant was it?"

"No!" Her hand flew up to clutch his. "I just wanted a stable, secure, happy life. I still do, especially now that I have a child. But I never wanted to be in a position where I'd have to rely on a man *financially.* That was why I was determined to have a career of my own."

Mack no longer seemed to be listening. He'd twisted around, using his free hand to dig into the cushion beside him. He pulled out a crumpled newspaper. "I noticed this earlier as I sat down. It's this morning's paper." He lifted a dark eyebrow. "Have you read it?"

"Not yet," she admitted, her heart giving a tiny

jump. "Priscilla gave it to me just before you came to pick me up, and I didn't have time. But she pointed out the article on Stephen Chaney, if that's what you're referring to. Is he a cousin of yours, Mack?" Her eyes glinted as something else struck her. "Are you secretly working for him? Is that what you haven't told me? Though why you'd want to keep it a secret..."

Mack's lip pursed in a rueful half smile. "If I'd known what I know now—if I'd known what you really wanted—I might have been more open with you, Suzie. I might even have agreed to have my photograph included in that newspaper article, as they wanted me to."

Suzie went still. "*Your* photograph?" Light dawned slowly. A blinding light. "You're saying—*you're* Stephen Chaney?"

"I'm afraid so."

She stared at him, finding it difficult to comprehend this amazing revelation. "And you decided to call yourself Stephen Chaney," she said slowly, a faint quaver in her voice, "because you didn't want me to know that you're now a millionaire computer whiz? You should have changed your surname as well, Mack," she chided shakily. "Chaney's not a common name. Prissy and I thought he'd have to be a cousin at least. I even wondered for a fleeting second if Stephen Chaney *could* be you."

"Only for a second?" Mack queried gently. "But you discounted the idea."

"Well, yes. I didn't think you would have become so rich and successful in such a short time without telling me. Or that you'd use a false name."

"It's not a false name. It's my real name. My full name is Stephen Mack Chaney. I was named Stephen after my father and Mack after my mother. But Mum dropped the Stephen—or Stevie, as I was back then—when my father walked out on us, and I've been Mack ever since. When I found out the truth about my father last year, I felt I owed it to him to call myself Stephen again—at least for business purposes. I was proud to."

"And partly to pull the wool over *my* eyes," Suzie suggested, "in the event of the media insisting on an interview? Mack, why was it so important to you to keep your success from me? I would have thought I'd be the first one you'd want to tell—once we met up again."

"Oh, I wanted to. Especially as I did it all for you." He caught her hand and pressed it to his lips. "I wanted to show you that I wasn't the irresponsible good-for-nothing you and your mother thought me. That I could make something of my life. But when the money and the success rolled in, I was afraid to tell you when I finally found you again. Afraid that if I did, you might think I was trying to *buy* you back, the way you thought I was doing the night I had that fluky win at the casino."

He pressed her hand to his rough cheek. "Before telling you about the success of Digger Software, I wanted to find out if I could win you back without using my money and sudden rise in the world to bribe you."

Suzie flinched. "I suppose it's my own fault you think I'm so mercenary!"

"No! No, Suzie, it's not that I thought you mercenary. The opposite. It was myself I wasn't sure of.

I wanted to know that I could win you back as *myself*—the Mack Chaney you used to know—not as the overnight millionaire whiz-kid calling himself Stephen Chaney. But I wanted you to know that I'd made at least *something* of my life, so I showed you my respectable new car and told you about the success of my new Internet Web editor. It's called Cobber, by the way. It's Digger Software's most successful product.''

''I think I'd better read this article,'' Suzie said shakily, and plucked it from him. She was silent for a few minutes. ''My goodness, Mack, it says Cobber is the most popularly downloaded Web-authoring tool in the *world*, with users in over a hundred countries! And your company, Digger Software, was founded in Sydney *a year ago*, though you've recently set up an office in Melbourne. A *year* ago?''

''I founded the company a few months after you walked out on me, Suzie—that last time.'' He gave a wry smile at the reminder that it hadn't been the first time she'd walked out on him. ''I'd already created Cobber, my Internet Web editor, several months before that, and it was doing so well I decided to form a company and expand into other products.''

Several months before she walked out on him? He'd already created his Web editor back *then?* She felt a rush of guilty shame. And she'd accused him, on their highly charged wedding night, of playing useless games and clinging to unrealistic pipe dreams!

''Oh, Mack, I'm sorry, I didn't know.'' She slipped her hand into his. ''Why didn't you tell me the night I—we—'' She flushed at the remembered images of that wildly passionate night.

Mack's mouth stretched in a grin. ''I did give you

a clue. I accused you of having little faith. But I didn't really want to tell you back then," he admitted, his dark eyes pleading for her understanding. "I wanted to make sure first that Cobber was going to be an ongoing success. And I wanted to set up my own company—a risky venture—and try to make a success of that, too, expanding into other software and employing staff to help me."

He gave her hand a squeeze. "Then, once I felt confident that the company was going to be sound, solid and successful, I intended to come for you—and make you eat your words. *Pipe dreams,*" he taunted. "*Useless games.*" His eyes were teasing now.

"Well, I eat humble pie," Suzie said happily. No wonder Mack was able to afford the best seats in the theater! She pursed her lips as she thought of something else. "That man you avoided at the casino the other night, Mack," she had no fear about asking anymore. "It wasn't because he was a bore, was it? It was because he knew you as Stephen Chaney—right?"

"Right." Mack looked chastened. "He works for me, as a matter of fact. He actually is a bit of a bore, socially, but as a programmer, he's the best."

"So are you likely to spring any more surprises on me?"

"Only in the bedroom, maybe." He eyed her hungrily. "Have I answered all your questions now?"

She nodded, then admonished gently, "Pity you didn't tell me all this before I agreed to marry Tristan Guthrie. If I'd known that you weren't a gambler or a serious drinker or the aimless biker my mother kept insisting you were, I would have ditched Tristan *before* our wedding day and you wouldn't have needed to come to my rescue."

"I was hoping you *would* ditch him before then—that you'd come to your senses in time." Mack glowered. "When I first heard you were planning to marry that gold-plated nerd, just as Cobber was starting to sell and show some promise—" He paused, a muscle working in the rugged line of his jaw, revealing the emotion he must have felt at the time.

"And then I found out that the jerk was married already." A satisfied glint speared his eye. "That was when I decided to fill out a notice of marriage form, hoping like hell that you'd fall back into my arms when you learned the truth." A smile tweaked his lips. "I never dreamed that I'd be able to persuade you to marry me on the spot, though."

"You can thank Jolie Fashions and the fashion media for that," she reminded him pertly. She wriggled a bit closer. "So it upset you, did it, knowing I was planning to marry Tristan Guthrie?" She ran a teasing finger up his arm and felt satisfaction as he shivered under her touch.

"That's putting it mildly," Mack growled. "I wondered how the hell I could compete with the golden boy from Guthrie Leather Goods. At that point in time I had nothing solid or secure to offer you. But I wasn't going to give up without a fight. I decided to check up on your smug-faced fiancé. I wanted to make sure he was good enough for you." He smirked. "He wasn't, of course."

"No, and I'll be eternally grateful to you, Mack, even though you took your time about exposing him." Suzie shuddered at the thought that she could have been married to Tristan by now if Mack hadn't uncovered his secret and put a stop to the wedding. And the ax could have fallen at any time during their marriage. Someone, sometime, would have found out about his first wife and exposed Tristan.

Mack pulled her into his arms, murmuring into her honeyed curls, "As soon as Katy's in the pink of health again and we find a house to live in, let's renew our marriage vows, Suzie."

Her heart fluttered. "Well, I don't know." She looked up at him, a teasing light in her eyes. "I'd pretty well decided not to get tied up with disgustingly rich men anymore."

"Not even for the sake of your fatherless child?" His tongue tickled her earlobe.

"Oh, well, for my child I'd do anything." She felt a shivery thrill run down her body. "Well, practically anything."

"*Practically* anything?"

"Well, I wouldn't go back to Tristan Guthrie, for starters. Or get tied up with any man I didn't love to pieces."

"Do you love *me* to pieces, by any chance?"

She smiled. "I do."

"And you'll marry me again? For keeps this time?"

"I will." She wound her arms round his neck. "Oh, Mack, yes, let's get married again. For keeps!"

"You'll be happy being married to a man who hates wearing a suit and tie?"

"I *love* black leather. And I like brown suede, too. I'll be happy being married to the man you are, Mack—the happiest woman, the happiest wife, in the world." Her voice shook. "And Katy's going to be the happiest daughter in the world to have a father like you."

"She already has the best mother." Mack's normally strong voice was deep and husky with emotion.

"And I—" he nuzzled his lips into the silky warmth of her throat, "already have the woman I've always wanted. You're going to make a beautiful bride all over again, Suzie—looking ravishing in one of your own creations, naturally."

"Naturally. And this time," Suzie vowed, holding him tight, "nothing in the world is going to prevent us staying together forever."

"Nothing?"

"Nothing."

Epilogue

They confirmed their wedding vows at a very private ceremony in the leafy garden of the comfortable double-storey home that Mack had bought for his new family. The house was within easy reach of Priscilla's boutique, though Suzie had decided to work mostly from home from now on, having converted a granny flat at the side of the house into a large sewing and designing room with a private fitting area.

With Mack and little Katy her priority now, and a new house to redecorate, Suzie had cut down her workload considerably, only taking on special assignments.

The latest was her own wedding gown.

She'd put far more loving care into this one than the elegant, highly publicized gown she'd designed for her aborted wedding to Tristan. The sorry gown that had ended up ruined and discarded on Mack's bathroom floor. She'd designed that first one for the sophisticated, smooth-haired Suzanne, winner of the

Australian Gown of the Year award, whereas this one she'd designed for the free-and-easy, fun-loving Suzie, curls and all—the real Suzie.

It was simplicity itself, sleeveless and scoop-necked—ideal for a midsummer's day—in pure white silk, with a delicate trail of embroidered flowers down the back of her skirt and along the hemline, her own fingers lovingly working each thread.

She wore no veil, instead weaving pale-pink rosebuds into her honey-gold curls, which tumbled in riotous disarray round her shoulders. Her only jewelry were the sapphire-and-diamond earrings Mack had given her as a wedding gift.

As she emerged from the house, clutching a simple posy of freshly picked roses in various shades of pink, music from the stereo hidden in the garden sprang to life, the romantic strains of "True Love" weaving through the warm summer air.

Mack was waiting in the garden with the marriage celebrant and the only other witnesses, Suzie's mother Ruth, Priscilla and Harry and their boys, and of course little Katy. Harry was the official photographer. There wasn't another camera in sight.

Mack had turned to face his bride, smiling as his dark eyes met hers. She smiled back, with all her love in her eyes.

Her mother was holding Katy, with Priscilla on hand to take over if Ruth tired of the jiggling bundle in her arms. Katy, healthily chubby again, had had no aftereffects from her dramatic illness and had made a complete recovery.

Suzie flashed a loving smile at her baby daughter, and another one at her mother—a smile with a touch of irony as she recalled Ruth's reaction to the phone call she'd made to her mother three months ago.

Ruth had been horrified when Suzie had told her she'd met up again with Mack Chaney and confirmed that he, not Tristan Guthrie, was the father of her beloved baby daughter. Ruth had been even more horrified when Suzie had announced that she and Mack were going to renew their marriage vows as soon as they'd found a house to live in.

"You're going to *stay* married to him? But he doesn't even have a decent job," her mother had wailed. "*Does* he?" she'd asked with little hope in her voice. She hadn't even waited for an answer. "Oh, Suzie, dear, I know you're doing well with your bridal gowns, but have you thought this through? Can you *afford* a new house?" Her deeper worry hung unspoken in the air: *Can you afford an irresponsible, dependent husband?*

"You obviously never read the business articles in the newspapers, Mum," Suzie had admonished, tongue in cheek, because she'd never bothered with them herself before Priscilla had handed her that newspaper article on Digger Software and its brilliant young founder. "I'll send you a writeup on Mack that was in the newspaper the other day. And by the way, for business purposes, Mack uses his first name, Stephen. Stephen Chaney."

Her mother had been totally mystified, but Suzie had refused to enlighten her, instead popping the article into the mail that same day. Two days later Ruth had called her back, stunned and delighted that the bad-boy biker who'd fathered her daughter's child had turned out to be so brilliantly clever. And so suddenly, miraculously, rich and famous.

"Still, he'll need to be careful," she'd warned Suzie, old suspicions dying hard. Her own painful experiences were still deeply ingrained. "Fortunes that are won quickly and easily can be lost in just the same way."

"Don't worry, Mum, Mack is a computer expert with a business and accounting degree behind him—he won't be doing anything stupid. He's nothing like—like Dad," Suzie assured her mother, knowing that was Ruth's greatest fear. "Mack doesn't gamble, he's not a big drinker, and he's sold his Harley. He drives a BMW now."

"A BMW!" That more than anything impressed Ruth. You didn't see too many no-hopers driving a BMW. The only car Ruth's family had ever possessed—a modest secondhand car—had had to be sold to pay off a gambling debt of her husband's.

"We were both very wrong about him, Mum," Suzie said soberly, regretting the months she'd lost with Mack—but then, he'd been busy founding his company and establishing himself, so she mightn't have seen much of him anyway. "You'll find that out when you get to know him properly."

But by the time Ruth arrived in Melbourne, she loved Mack already. She even thanked him for saving Suzie from making the mistake of her life.

"I pushed Suzie into that near-disastrous wedding with Tristan Guthrie," she admitted in a wobbly voice. "I knew Suzie didn't love him the way she loved you, Mack. But I thought that respect and security and a rich, reliable husband would make her happier in the long run than uncertainty and struggle. But love is the most important thing after all, isn't it?"

Ruth's eyes were misty. Her own love for Suzie's tortured father might have faltered on many occasions, but it had never died, sustaining her through the darkest times. And it sustained her still, even stronger now that he was gone and the pain and torment were behind her.

"Yes, Mum," Suzie agreed, her eyes dancing because she knew that Mack's newfound fame and fortune, and his swanky BMW, had added a special luster to her mother's vision of him. "Love is the most important thing."

And Mack's eyes were telling her the same thing now, as she joined him in the garden. They didn't need his millions or his fame or a swanky car. They only needed each other and Katy. As it was, Mack had given a lot of his money away already to needy charities, and had invested a sizable proportion for Katy's education and future, knowing that security was so important to Suzie.

"Even if Digger Software crashes tomorrow," he'd told her, "Katy's future is assured. And we're both capable of getting other jobs, you especially, my talented darling. You could launch your own label now if you wanted to."

"Later, perhaps," she'd answered with a happy sigh. "For a while I just want you and Katy and some not-too-demanding bridal assignments, and maybe a few more babies to fill all those bedrooms upstairs...."

"Well, maybe I can help with that last one," Mack had responded with a wicked glint in his eye, and he'd been helping to fulfil that particular wish every night since.

As they renewed their wedding vows before the

local celebrant, Suzie wondered with a trembly thrill if Mack could read the special secret in her eyes. She'd only confirmed it that morning, after buying a pregnancy test from the chemist.

She wondered dreamily if Mack would want a boy this time. A baby brother for Katy would be wonderful. But a baby sister, another precious little girl, would be just as wonderful.

Her eyes clung to Mack's as they declared their love for each other. She drank in the deep love that glowed in the warm black depths, and knew with a wave of sheer happiness, that life could never get any better than this.

"I'll love you forever, Mack," she whispered. *For ever and ever and ever,* her glistening eyes told him.

And she basked in the radiant answering love that enveloped her.

* * * * *